ALTERED SENSE

Printed in Australia
Cover design by Shawline Publishing Group Pty Ltd
Images in this book are copyright approved for Shawline Publishing Group Pty Ltd
Illustrations within this book are copyright approved for Shawline Publishing Group Pty Ltd

First Printing: May 2023
Shawline Publishing Group Pty Ltd
www.shawlinepublishing.com.au
Paperback ISBN 978-1-9227-5109-6
Ebook ISBN 978-1-9229-9312-0

Distributed by Shawline Distribution and Lightningsource Global

A catalogue record for this book is available from the National Library of Australia

More great Shawline titles can be found here:

New titles also available through Books@Home Pty Ltd.
Subscribe today - www.booksathome.com.au

ALTERED SENSE

MAX JEFFRIES

For Morgan.

*For believing in me from the very first idea,
to the completion of this story.*

*I would like to thank my parents for their valuable and
trusted insights which helped create this novel.*

ONE

A strong breeze sliced through the air, forcing Will to push on harder as he walked home from his late shift. The night seemed darker than usual. A shiver crawled up his spine when he looked up and saw that many of the streetlights weren't working. It was winter in Sydney, and even with streetlights, the crisp evenings felt darker than the warm summer nights.

As he battled on, pulling his thick jacket up high around his neck, he made his way through the streets lined with small townhouses as fast as he could. He walked his usual route home, which took him far from the bright lights of the hospital where he worked, through to the quiet residential streets. The wind slapped his pale face, which was reddening as blood rushed to the surface, trying to keep him warm.

Ahead, Will heard yelling, swearing and the smashing of glass. He carefully looked up, hoping not to bring any attention to himself. Glancing in the direction of the noise, he saw two men and a woman. Teenagers in fact, no older than sixteen or seventeen. They were huddled together in front of a poorly-lit apartment building, wearing brightly-coloured jumpers and trackpants, smoking cigarettes and shoving each other, laughing loudly.

Will picked up his pace, head down, trying to avoid their gaze. The smashed glass looked like it'd once belonged to beer bottles. The teens must've already finished several, from the way they were yelling and stumbling around. Will preferred to avoid strangers at the best of times, so he crossed the road and passed them as quickly as he could. Regardless if they were looking for trouble or not, he knew for a fact that he wasn't. He was tall, just a little over six feet, but scrawny, with spindly arms. He knew his best defence was to avoid any confrontation altogether, so he pressed on and kept his eyes fixed on the path in front of him.

As he passed the group, he felt himself relax. They hadn't even seemed to notice him, and remained on their side of the road, chatting amongst themselves. He felt pretty foolish for assuming kids hanging out on the street at night wanted to start trouble. After all, he was a teenager once, and even now at 27 years old, had never raised a fist at anyone. But then, he'd also never smoked a cigarette or drank in the streets. If he'd picked a fight in his youth, it wouldn't have ended in his favour.

A loud voice called behind him.

'Hey, you!'

It was one of the drunk teens. He flinched, his stomach flipping, but ignored the voice and kept walking.

The same voice called out again.

'Don't walk away from me. Come here, I just want a smoke.'

Will turned. The two boys were approaching him, while the girl sat in the gutter, drinking.

'I don't smoke,' he called back, trying to sound more confident than he was. He pulled his jacket tighter and kept walking.

'What did you say to me?' one said, as he caught up, coming uncomfortably close to Will. Neither of them was taller than him, but they were stocky, rugged, and very drunk.

'I said I don't smoke,' Will replied feebly. His hands shook, and he hid them in his pockets.

As he turned to leave, one of the teens, who had a flat, broad nose covered in freckles, moved directly in front of him. The stench of alcohol on his breath was putrid, and all Will wanted to do was end the conversation as quickly as he could. The teen glared directly into Will's eyes, then gave him a cheeky smirk.

'You got any money for us to buy some, then?'

The other teen stood beside Will, grinning crookedly, showing yellow teeth behind thin lips.

'I don't, sorry.' Will looked down at his feet. His way forward was still blocked, and his heart was pounding. This situation was about to get really bad, really soon. 'Look, guys, I've had a long day at work. I don't have any money, or anything… but yeah, have a good night.'

Again, he tried to walk away, but the teens refused to back down.

'Don't lie to me,' the freckled teen said, still standing way too close to Will's face. 'You've got cash, I know it. Let's have some.'

A wave of panic hit Will and his throat clogged. Fight or flight was kicking in, but he knew flight was his strength. Would they catch him if he ran?

'No,' he managed.

Without warning, the freckled teen threw a clenched fist toward his face. It hit him straight in the nose. His head snapped backward, and he gasped as the hot sting of the punch took his breath away. Before he could react, the other charged into his back. Then he was on the ground, the two teens standing over him, kicking him as hard as they could.

Will lost count of the strikes. All he could do was curl into the foetal position and try to protect his vital body parts. Through the barrage of blows, he could hear laughter and taunts being hurled at him. Between two particularly brutal kicks to his ribcage, the freckled teen told the other to look through his pockets.

Blood pooled on the concrete. The pain was like nothing he had ever endured. Another hard punch collided with the side of his face, and dark dots appeared in his vision, as the bloodstained concrete under his face began to fade out to blackness.

***

The girl, who'd remained in the gutter, got up and approached her friends, zipping up her orange hoodie.

'Did you get some cash?' she asked, prodding Will's limp body with her foot.

'He didn't have any,' the freckled teen said.

'Alright, that's enough, then. Let's go. Someone's gonna hear us,' she called.

'Get out of here, then,' the thin-mouthed teen shouted back between kicks.

A terrace porch light turned on. The middle-aged resident ran out, holding a golf club.

'I've called the police! I'm sick of you kids carrying on.' He bounded toward the road, the club raised over his head. He was heavyset and muscular, charging toward them with his fists clenched.

'Then put the club down, and let's go, big guy,' the freckled teen said.

'Don't try that tough act on me,' he replied, charging onward. As he got nearer, he glimpsed the young man lying face-down, surrounded by his own blood. He'd heard the yelling, but didn't know a fight had broken out.

'Jesus,' he said. 'What have you done?' He dropped the club and ran over to Will's limp body.

'Come on, let's get out of here,' the girl said, tugging desperately on her friends' arms.

The three ran down the street until they were hidden by darkness. Kneeling, the man examined the mess before him. Will's face was so swollen and discoloured it looked as though he was in anaphylaxis. Although he'd regained slight consciousness, he seemed close to losing it again. His breathing was laboured, gurgling with the blood that leaked into his mouth.

'Stay still.' The man cradled Will's head, moving him into the recovery position. 'It'll be okay. We'll get you to hospital.'

In the distance, sirens sounded.

TWO

The ambulance sped into the City South Hospital's emergency driveway, meeting a waiting team of nurses. As they unloaded Will from the van, the paramedics helped wheel his stretcher inside.

'BP is 103/62 and dropping, heart rate 110. Looks like some internal bleeding,' one paramedic called out.

'He's in and out of consciousness, but breathing on his own,' said the other.

'Geez, Will, what happened? Let's get him stable quickly,' said Doctor Michelle Stone. 'You'll be okay – just hang on. Get him up to Trauma Bay One. I'm paging the team now.'

The nurses wheeled Will toward the trauma unit. Along the way, they refreshed his bandages, doing their best to keep his blood pressure steady and manage the bleeding.

Two police officers arrived just as Will was being brought into the ICU. Given the number of Friday and Saturday night assaults in the city, they were familiar with the hospital, along with most of the triage staff and their protocols. The first rule: walk and talk – fast.

Constable Maybury, a tall, broad-chested 21-year-old with a dark crew-cut hairstyle, tried to keep up with Doctor Stone. 'How is he?'

'He's in a pretty bad way. I just saw him half an hour ago, on his way out for the night. It's horrible this happened to him. Any idea who did it, or why?'

She strode through the emergency department, tapping on a tablet. Both officers did their best to keep up.

'Sounds like a bunch of kids jumped him, then took off when a neighbour chased them. We have a few officers out looking for them now. He was lucky the neighbour came out before it got much worse.'

'Geez, poor Will.' Doctor Stone shook her head. Looking down at Will's injured face, she brushed his thick mop of dark messy hair away from his forehead, but quickly composed herself and returned to her professional persona.

'Look, guys,' she continued, 'there's no point in you waiting around here. Let us get him treated and stable. Judging by the look of things, he won't be going anywhere soon. Maybe come back and try to speak with him later.'

'Sure,' Maybury replied. 'Call us if anything changes. I imagine the detectives will call in tomorrow.'

By the time he finished, Doctor Stone was long gone, straight to the trauma ward to ensure Will was seen to immediately. She hoped the busy night would settle down, but for now, patients continued to pile in quicker than they could be attended to. She expected a rough night ahead.

***

Rosie Kennedy's phone woke her just after midnight. A junior doctor from the emergency room had been tasked with calling Will's registered next of kin, and he knew from experience there was no benefit to beating around the bush. He gave Rosie the news efficiently but sympathetically. Through the horrified yelps on the other end of the phone, he related all the details and Will's current status. As Rosie heard what happened to her little brother, panic surged through her entire body. She fired off questions quicker than the doctor could answer them.

'What do you mean, attacked? Is he conscious? Oh, God, where is he now?'

The doctor tried his best to calm Rosie down by telling her that her brother was in capable hands, and in a stable condition. He resolved the call with good news: that Will would be moved out of the intensive care unit quicker than they'd expected.

Aside from her husband Ben and four-year-old daughter Claire, Will was Rosie's only family. Their mother had passed away two years ago from chronic heart disease, and neither of them had seen their father since Will was a baby. Although Rosie had left the city years ago, she still looked out for him, and they spoke at least once a week.

Rosie crept into Claire's room and kissed her softly on the forehead, before racing down the hall, grabbing her keys, and beginning the long drive toward City South Hospital.

***

Will woke up in a hospital bed around 2 a.m. His head felt like it was ripping apart, and he was overcome by wave after wave of nausea. Every shallow breath he took was agonising. Despite never having broken a rib before, he knew at least one must've been cracked. At the end of the bed, a plastic bag contained what looked like his blood-stained hospital uniform. He held his breath as he tried to sit himself up a little more, but the thumping in his head told him to stay still.

Doctor Ravi Sandeep entered the room and went straight for the vital signs monitors. He wasn't Will's assigned doctor, but as soon as he'd heard about what happened, he'd taken the time out of his busy night to check up on him. Will groaned as he tried to lift his head, and Ravi hurried over to carefully press him back down onto the bed.

'Will, It's Ravi. Stay still. You've got a concussion, some pretty nasty bruising, and a couple of cracked ribs.'

'Am I gonna be okay?'

Will gasped and clenched his teeth at how painful it was to string those five words together.

'We're waiting on the results from some scans, but things are looking good for now. Just sleep, okay? You need rest.' Ravi placed a small device linked to a cable on Will's stomach. 'If the pain creeps up again, press this. It'll give you some relief.'

As soon as Will added the liquid to the IV line, he was immediately pain-free, and fast asleep.

THREE

Will had been working at the hospital from its beginning, so he'd become something of a reliable fixture around the place. That had earned him some respect as the go-to maintenance guy. During his tenure, he'd also developed a good friendship with Ravi, one of the younger doctors in the psychiatric unit. Aside from his older sister, Ravi was his only real friend. At first, Will had thought Ravi was just being polite when he'd invited him for lunch one day, but they'd gotten along well, and found they shared a common interest in online gaming.

Like Will, Ravi was tall, thin, and introverted. He wore thick glasses with black rims, which he would constantly adjust while he was speaking. He didn't wear scrubs or a lab coat. Rather, he wore a simple shirt, tie and trousers, and kept his hair in a crew cut.

As Will slept, Ravi made sure the nurses remained attentive to his monitors, and found time in his own busy schedule to stop by every hour to make sure his friend was recovering properly.

***

As the morning sunlight filtered through cracks in the hospital curtains, Will woke in an unfamiliar room. He must've slept for several hours, but his body still ached. He lay awake, barely able to open his eyes, grateful for the painkillers sparing him more agony than his body could've managed. On the downside, they didn't seem to agree with his stomach. A wave of nausea followed every dose he received.

He remembered most of what happened leading up to his attack, and the first several punches and kicks. Everything after that, including his ride to the hospital, was hazy.

Will looked to his right and saw Rosie sitting by his bedside. Even though he was groggy from the painkillers, he could make out her thin body, long dark hair, and pointed nose. His slight movement made her spin and grab his hand.

'Hey, it's me. You're okay. The doctors were in while you were still asleep – they told me what happened, but said you'll be alright. They did some scans and couldn't see any serious damage.'

Will slowly nodded and squeezed his sister's hand.

'I'm so happy you're awake. Just stay still, everything will be alright.' She gave a wide smile. He saw her eyes were bloodshot, and there was a tissue in her hand. He could only imagine how frightened she must've been.

A short time later, a nurse he didn't recognise came in with a carton of juice.

'Welcome back, Mr Denham. You had us all worried there for a while.' She smiled as she got closer to his bed. 'Here, try to have some juice. A doctor will be in soon to check up on you.' She checked the monitors, before quietly leaving the room.

With some help from Rosie, Will managed a couple of hands-free sips. While he lay there in silence, he remembered the terror from last night, and it seemed to replicate itself again. Although he knew he'd be safe while at the hospital, his body still trembled. He felt more frightened than ever.

Slowly, he tried to look at the bag of bloody clothes still hanging off the end of his bed. The kids had probably emptied his pockets, but he wanted to see what may have been left behind. Looking to his side, he saw his phone on the bedside table, and although the screen was cracked, he was relieved to know they hadn't taken it. He found out the hard way that sitting up still wasn't possible, as his insides clenched, his chest tightening around his aching ribs. He groaned and fell back into the bed. Dizzy from the movement and the medications, he vomited all over his hospital gown.

The nurse rushed back into the room.

'You've got to stay still, I mean it,' she said. 'You won't be doing yourself any favours by moving about.' She tutted at Will as she began gently wiping down his chest and gown.

'Sorry,' he replied, face red.

'Don't worry about it. It's my job.'

'I'm just trying to make sense of what happened,' Will said. He attempted to take control of the clean-up, but the nurse brushed him away.

'Now, I just spoke to some detectives,' she said. 'They want to come and talk to you later, if you can remember what happened, and the doctor says it's okay.'

'I know what happened. I just want to know why.'

The nurse ignored him and packed up the soiled towels before walking toward the door. She was probably the stereotypical busy, no-nonsense nurse. Overworked and underpaid.

Just as she reached the door, she turned back to Will. Her body language shifted, and she appeared a little softer.

'I'm sorry this happened to you,' she said.

'What's your name?' Will asked. 'I haven't seen you before.'

'Jenny. I just transferred here a couple of weeks ago.'

'Thanks for looking after me,' he said, as he tried to smile.

'No problem. I heard you work in maintenance here.' She moved back into the room and straightened up Will's blanket.

'Yeah. Speaking of maintenance, can you do me a favour?'

Jenny shook her head and raised a hand. 'Don't worry. Your

team's heard about what happened.'

'No, not that. My uniform.' Will pointed to the blood-soaked clothes still in sight at the end of his bed. 'Can you just throw that out? I don't want to look at it.'

'Of course. Now get some rest.' She looked over at Rosie. 'Make sure he doesn't move too much.'

For the next couple of hours, Will drifted in and out of a broken sleep, plagued by horrific nightmares. First, he dreamt of explosions happening throughout City South Hospital. The dream became more vivid as he explored the wards and corridors, wearing only the hospital gown he'd fallen asleep in. As he crept through the wrecked building, his ears filled with a high-pitched ringing. Though he was afraid, he had no control over his legs. They continued to drive him through the seemingly endless hallways, toward the centre of the hospital. The air was heavy with sulphur and concrete dust, which waited to settle on the crushed ground.

The last thing he remembered was entering a large patient ward, to see a mass of charred bodies. He woke up quickly, in a full-body sweat, struggling to catch his breath. He stared at the ceiling, trying to forget what he'd seen.

When his body finally shut down again, he dreamt he was in a dirty, poorly-lit garage, standing at a wooden workbench. The bench was scattered with metal parts, and he was holding a thin yellow wire. He unscrewed the metal cap of a small tube, pushed the wire inside, and felt its tip reach something spongy. A digital display on the workbench lit up with the word Active. He removed the wire from the tubing, and the display switched off.

His dream shifted. Suddenly, he was back in the ward, surrounded by wreckage and death. The room was frighteningly quiet. All the beds were empty, but looked like they'd been slept in. He began searching the rest of the ward, desperate to locate any survivors. As he turned down a hallway, he was confronted by a tunnel of fire, creeping toward him. Shrapnel was propelled by the flames as they filled the hallway. The combustion was occurring in slow motion, but Will was trapped. His legs refused to work, and he had no way to protect himself. He watched as the massive fireball moved closer to him. Just as he was about to be engulfed, he woke in another full-body sweat.

The dreams had felt so real. As he tried to relax his body and slow his breathing, the pain in his head and body crept back.

'Are you okay?' Rosie asked. 'You've been groaning and moving around for a while now.'

'Yeah,' he replied groggily. 'Bad dreams.' He fumbled for his painkiller switch and pressed the button, injecting himself with sweet relief.

Will spent the rest of the morning between broken naps and intense pain. Later in the day, a doctor in dark-blue scrubs under a white coat entered the room.

'How are you feeling?'

Like Will, Doctor Stone had worked at the hospital since it opened. She was a tall, middle-aged woman, with tan skin and brown hair tied in a small ponytail that just touched her lab coat. They'd crossed paths many times, but never had a reason to speak before.

'I feel like a train's hit me. And I'm pretty dizzy.'

'That'd be the concussion. You took some nasty hits, but you got here quickly. You have two cracked ribs, a broken nose, and some bruising, but I'm glad to say you'll be okay. The bleeding stopped faster than we expected. We'll keep you on the antibiotics as a precaution, though your cuts and grazes are clean, and I don't expect any infection now.'

Doctor Stone glanced over the IV line and the monitors. She returned to the end of Will's bed and crossed her arms.

'Do you remember what happened?'

'Yeah, I do. But it happened so quickly. A bunch of kids jumped me after asking for a cigarette.'

'Well, after a couple of days' rest here, you'll be okay to go,' she said.

She listened to Will's chest, felt his arms, shoulders, and neck, then made notes on a tablet.

'There are police officers outside, who want to talk to you. Are you happy to chat with them?'

Will nodded and Doctor Stone left the room to call them in.

After trying his best to sit up a little more, he lost the fight with his body. He gave up, and settled for raising his head. Moments later, two smartly-dressed detectives entered the room. One was an athletic woman in her late twenties, attractive in fitted charcoal pants and a loose white blouse. Her blonde hair was tied back in a tight bun, with not one loose strand visible. Her skin was pale and smooth, and her wide smile showed a set of perfectly straight teeth. The male detective who followed her was older, maybe forty. He was at least six feet tall, with a broad chest and wearing a well-fitted navy suit. Will had never met any actual detectives before, but thought those two were good-looking enough to play police on TV.

'Hi, Will. I'm Detective Senior Constable Woods, and this is Detective Senior Constable Lapis,' the female officer said, with a soft smile. She looked at Rosie, who stood next to Will's bed. 'You mind if we have a chat alone?'

'I think it's best if I stay here,' Rosie said sternly.

'It's okay, I'll be fine. Maybe get yourself a coffee,' Will said, waving her away.

She nodded, and looked both detectives up and down.

'I'll be back soon,' she said, as she left the room. Woods closed the door behind her.

'So, how are you feeling?' Woods asked.

'Terrible,' Will replied. 'It's the worst headache I've ever had.'

'It must have been a nasty attack. That's why we're here – we want to find out who did this to you,' Woods said. 'Are you able to run us through everything that happened?'

'Sure.' Will tried again to sit more upright. He recounted the entire event without interruption from either detective. They took notes, listened attentively, and paid him exceptional courtesy. Once he'd told them everything he could remember, they asked clarifying questions, and honed in on a detailed description of the attackers.

When they'd finished their questions, they thanked Will and packed up their notes.

'Listen,' Woods said, 'I've been around long enough to see too many of these attacks. You need to take care of yourself.'

'Yeah. They have me on meds, and I'm bandaged up. Should only be a couple of days here,' Will replied.

'That's not what I meant.'

She handed him two business cards. One was her own, with her contact information at the Surry Hills Detectives Office. The second was a victim's information card.

'You should check these people out. It's a victim support group – you can go to a meeting, or they can put you in touch with a psychologist. It helps, trust me.'

'Sure, thanks,' Will said. By the sincere look on her face, he knew she meant every word.

'Well, we have your information, and will be in touch soon with any updates on the case,' Woods said.

Once both detectives had left, Will examined the first card. Aubrey Woods – Detective Senior Constable. It listed her phone number, station details, and email. The second card read Pitt Street Victim Support Group – United in Strength, and had a phone number and website. He placed it on the side table, before drifting back to sleep.

When he woke in the early hours of the afternoon, Rosie had returned to the chair beside his bed.

'You must be tired,' he said, noticing the bags under her eyes.

'Don't worry about me.' She shrugged, stretching her back. 'You're the one who needs the rest.'

'I'll be okay here. I'm not going anywhere tonight, anyway – why don't you stay at my place tonight? You can't get a decent sleep in a chair.'

'Might be a good idea… that way, you can be stuck with me for longer after I've had a good sleep.'

'Take the keys from that bag there,' he said, pointing toward the end of the bed. 'The nurses told me the kids didn't take them.'

Rosie gave Will a kiss on the forehead.

'I'll give Ben a call, and let him know you're okay.'

'Great, thanks. I'll talk to him soon myself. Don't trash my place, please.'

'If it's anything like the last time I was there, you've already done that yourself. I'll be back soon. Don't go anywhere.'

Will smiled. It really meant a lot to him she'd made the trip to be there. It was also refreshing that she'd felt comfortable enough to relax a little and try to cheer him up, after she'd known he'd make a full recovery. Once she'd left, he stared up at the white ceiling, battling with his headache until he fell asleep.

The dreams continued. Will found himself in his hospital bed, alone. This time, however, there was no death, no wreckage. He walked through the deserted, silent hospital, the only noise the sound of his bare feet slapping against the cold floor. As he approached the exit, his whole body tightened. He tried to leave through the sliding glass doors, but his legs wouldn't allow it. Continuing past the exit, he made his way to the back of the hospital, to see if he could leave by the rear loading dock. He could hear a faint ticking noise, which got louder the further he went. When he could see the loading dock entrance at the end of a long corridor, the ticking became louder. He reached to open the door, and as his palm touched it, an explosion forced him to the ground. Debris and smoke surrounded him. As though time was drifting slowly, the ceiling and walls started to collapse. Just before he was buried under the rubble, he woke up with his head aching.

Even in his sleep, he was frightened. He hoped he could stay awake.

FOUR

Later in the night, Ravi came to visit Will.

'Hey, buddy. How are you feeling?'

'I'm still sore, but I've slept all day, so that helped. My head's still throbbing, though.'

'That's all pretty normal.' Ravi flipped through some paperwork on a clipboard he was carrying. 'The rehab notes say you were moving well today. I spoke with the day shift, and they're pleased with your progress.'

Ravi went back to his notes. However, he couldn't avoid his curiosity for long.

'So, what happened?'

'I don't know. I mean, it all happened pretty fast. I was walking home, and a couple of guys jumped me. They asked for a smoke, but the more I think about it… whether I gave them one or not, the result would've been the same. They were drunk, and I was just there. An easy target, I guess.'

'Do they think the cops will find them? Like, do these types of things actually get solved much?'

'I hope so,' Will replied. 'I mean, I can't undo what's happened to me, but they shouldn't get away with it. Who knows, they might even attack someone else.' Gazing out the small window, he took a deep breath. 'Or me again. I mean, they know me now. They'd be able to recognise me.'

That was the first time he'd thought about the possibility of a second attack. They'd attacked him close to home, and they knew what he looked like. He felt sick, suddenly, and not from the concussion or medication.

'You know, you're welcome to stay at my place for a while,' Ravi said. 'If you want to stay away from the area.'

'Thanks, Ravi. I appreciate that, I really do, but I think I just want to move on and get back to normal. I'll be okay.'

Though he said that, he'd already started planning to put money aside for rideshares when he resumed late shifts, to save taking the same walk home.

'Alright. I better get ready for my shift, but I'll come and check up on you later.'

Will gave a thumbs-up as Ravi left the room.

Around 7 p.m., Will was served some lukewarm pumpkin soup. It was sensible for the hospital to have avoided serving him a steaming hot meal, because he dribbled most of the first painful spoonful down his chin. As he wiped himself down, careful to avoid his bruised chest, Rosie came back into the room, looking a bit more relaxed.

'I updated Ben, but haven't told Claire anything yet. I don't want to frighten her.'

'Good idea. Did you get some rest?'

'I did. Thanks for letting me use your place, but would it kill you to clean up once in a while? I was sneezing the whole time. Everything was dusty.'

Will rolled his eyes, and Rosie grinned.

'I think if you vacuumed that place, you'd find the brown carpet is actually white,' she continued.

'I like my place just fine how it is, thank you very much.' Will laughed softly, to avoid disturbing his bandaged ribs.

'Any idea when you can get out of here? I hope they won't force you back to work too soon,' Rosie said, as she walked over to look at Will's dinner.

'Not sure yet – it's not up to me. Maybe after a little more rehab to make sure I'm moving right. I'm feeling better, though.'

'Well, I'll hang around until you're back on your feet.' Rosie sat by the bed and stared out the window. The haze of the city lights prevented her from seeing the stars she was familiar with, living outside Sydney.

Later in the evening, just as he was about to doze off again, Ravi returned to the room. After introducing himself to Rosie, he gave Will a big smile.

'I asked to deliver the good news. Your scan's clear, and you've got no infection. Your nose and ribs will heal up, and though the bruising will look worse before it looks better, you can go home tomorrow afternoon. The physical therapists just want to spend a little time with you in the morning, make sure you aren't too stiff.'

'Sounds good,' Will said weakly.

'I can stay with you for a bit, if you like,' Rosie said, as she placed a hand on top of Will's.

'No, I'll be okay. I can't hide forever, and I'm sure it'll all be fine.'

'You'll still have to take it slowly, but we'll give you some painkillers,' Ravi said. 'And that reminds me – we got a memo from the administration department. They're going to have a chat with you tomorrow, but it sounds like they won't rush you back to work.'

Will nodded, and Rosie rubbed his shoulder.

'Anyway, it's flat out tonight. I better run. Nice to meet you, Rosie. Talk soon, Will.'

As Ravi left the room, Rosie hugged Will. He winced and recoiled.

'Oh, sorry,' she said. 'I was just so scared when I heard you were in here.'

'I still haven't processed it all myself,' he replied, sinking deeply into his pillow.

'Well, let's hope the police find these people, and they get what they deserve.'

Rosie stayed with Will until midnight, then left to his apartment. The ward was quiet, and he slept through the entire night, with no more nightmares.

The next morning, Rosie woke him bright and early. She wanted to help with his breakfast, but he was feeling well enough to manage himself. While the bruises on his arms and body were looking rough, he felt a little more mobile. He made the mistake of asking for Rosie's makeup mirror. His nose was almost twice its usual size. Even under the heavy bandages, he could see the swelling and redness. Rosie told him it had been reset well, and was looking better than it had yesterday.

Later in the day, he was visited by Lenore Hill, the hospital's administration manager and his boss. She was almost 65, but had no plans on slowing down. She always wore brightly-coloured blazers, and red lipstick to match her short red hair. Normally, she was bubbly and chatty. Today, however, she couldn't hide how sad she was. He wasn't used to people feeling sorry for him. It was an odd experience.

'I'm so sorry this happened, Will. And on your way home from work! It's just awful.'

'Thanks, Lenore. So, about work...'

'Don't worry about that for now,' she said, with a warm smile. 'Take a couple of weeks off, and look after yourself. I don't want you to feel rushed. The hospital board knows what happened, and seeing as you were on your way home from work, we'll be paying you sick leave while you're away.'

This surprised him. Lenore likely would've spent the morning arguing with the board to get him taken care of financially. All the staff knew the hospital didn't treat them with the same level of compassion as they did their patients.

Lenore handed Will a large card. It was signed by the hospital staff, including everyone in the maintenance department. After he thanked her, and she left, he began reading all the positive messages from his colleagues.

Between doctors and nurses looking in on him as part of their official duties, Will also had a few informal visits from staff. Some passed on their best wishes for a speedy recovery, and some gave their condolences, but were clearly just curious about how he looked, all swollen and bandaged.

Following a final rehabilitation session in the early afternoon, Will was officially discharged. When he left the hospital with Rosie, the first breath of fresh air felt good, despite his bruised and cracked ribs. Although he was glad to be leaving, he couldn't help but feel slightly anxious upon seeing the road where he started his usual walking route, which had ended so badly just a few nights ago.

Everything in Will's one-bedroom apartment was how he'd left it – only a little tidier, thanks to Rosie. Most of the appliances in the kitchen were outdated, and the furniture scattered around the open-plan living and dining room didn't match. The only modern items in his apartment were the TV, computer, and modem. His place was too small for two people, so he assured Rosie he'd be okay. After making sure everything at the apartment was in order, Rosie gave him a long hug, and promised to call him first thing the following morning.

When she left, Will made his way to the kitchen. His mood lifted a little when he saw she'd bought groceries while he was in hospital. After he ate, he took some painkillers, before falling asleep in his old armchair.

He woke up several hours later with his heart pounding against his chest. Looking out the small window, he guessed it was around midnight. His apartment was quiet, the usual hum of evening traffic gone. His sleep had been deep and peaceful, but his body was radiating heat. When he stood, he stumbled, dizzy and aching.

The apartment had no air conditioning, so he dragged himself to the bathroom to stand on the cool tiles and splash water on his face. By the time he reached it, he was down to his underwear, and had left a trail of sweat-soaked clothes behind him. He gripped the sides of the sink, staring at his reflection in the mirror above. He lifted the bandage off his nose, which was damp with sweat. The bruising was still deep blue. His dark hair was so wet it appeared he'd just got out of the shower. Several strands were stuck to his forehead.

While the tap ran, Will did his best to wipe himself down with a bath towel. He wondered whether he had a fever, or was experiencing some after-effects of the concussion. He'd never had such an injury before, so didn't know what the recovery process was like, but none of his doctors had told him to watch for sudden and intense full-body sweats.

When the sink was full, he plunged his head all the way into the frigid water. His body relaxed, immediately feeling a little cooler. He resurfaced and began splashing the back of his neck. As he bent to collect another handful, he jumped back and threw himself into the bathroom wall.

Tongues of flames licked the water. He forgot about his bruised and broken body as he watched bright flames engulf the sink. The heat was intense, and he felt out of breath. Oxygen was draining from the bathroom. He threw his wet, sweat-soaked towel over the growing flames.

The towel did nothing. The fire manoeuvred around it and crept down the sink, toward the bathroom tiles. The bathroom mirror was covered in steam, and Will could no longer see his own reflection. As the flames continued to grow, he made out the word Help drawn upon the mirror, as though a finger had traced the letters.

His throat knotted with terror. Nothing could cause the fire to move the way it was – as if it were alive, crawling along the walls like a spider. It spread to the doorway, trapping him inside. The only window was to the left of the sink, close to the ceiling. It was far too small for him to slide through. As he crouched in the corner, trying to find a way out, he heard a woman screaming.

At first, Will thought it must've been his elderly next-door neighbour, Mrs Simmons. But as the screaming continued, he realised it wasn't coming from her apartment.

It was coming from his own bathroom. From within the flames themselves.

The voice shouted in a drawn-out echo.

'Please, someone! Help!'

Will cowered in the corner as the flames engulfed the bathroom, moving closer toward him. In a moment of clarity, he crawled toward the bathtub, pulled himself inside, and kept low. He peered around, looking for his wet towel. Though the fire persisted, he couldn't see any smoke, or any structural damage.

Suddenly, the flames whipped violently toward Will. He let out one loud scream as he braced for the blaze to consume him.

FIVE

Will woke to the sound of his phone ringing loudly from the living room. Sunshine poured through the small bathroom window, reflecting from the mirror above the sink and beaming directly into his eyes. He was still inside the bathtub, tangled in the baby-blue shower curtains.

To add to the trauma of his recent assault, his body now ached even more from sleeping in the porcelain tub. It was agonising to lift his stiff body up. He didn't know what had happened the night before. The fire had stopped, and his bathroom was intact. He couldn't find any explanation for what had happened, and his mind continued to replay the fire with intense clarity. It had felt so real...

Quickly, Will walked to the living room and picked up his ringing phone. It was Rosie.

'Hey,' he said.

'I just wanted to check up on you. Did you sleep okay?'

'Had a few bad dreams, I guess. I'm still sore.' Will rubbed his forehead. He felt distracted, but decided he wouldn't talk to Rosie about the fire, and have her worry.

'Do you want to say hi to Claire?'

'Maybe later... I'm not feeling the best.'

'Well, I'll let you go then. Eat something, okay? And take it easy. Call if you need anything.'

'Will do. Thanks, Rosie.'

Will ended the call. He tried to calm down and rationally process what had happened last night, but thoughts flooded his mind. How could there be a fire in his bathroom, with no apparent cause? How was he still alive? Why wasn't the building evacuated? Where was the damage?

As he dressed, he thought about the screaming he'd heard. Given how loud it was, Mrs Simmons must've heard it too. He wanted to check up on her, as their two bathrooms were back-to-back, separated only by a thin wall. Maybe she'd seen the same thing, and had some sort of explanation for him. He'd lived in the old apartment building for three years, while she must've been there for at least 30. Usually, he kept to himself, with little more than a polite nod here and there to the other residents. However, Mrs Simmons was a lonely, widowed old lady who'd trap him in conversation whenever she could. He felt sorry for her, and occasionally indulged her by having tea in her apartment. He enjoyed the company, but never initiated it himself.

It took a while for Mrs Simmons to get to the door. When she did, she had a strange look of relief, exhaling deeply as she beamed at him. Will gave a strained smile in return, overwhelmed by the musky, excessive perfume she wore, mixed with the scent of the stale potpourri she had scattered around her apartment.

'Oh, William, it's fantastic to see you,' she said. 'I spoke to your sister a couple of days ago, when she was staying here, and she told me what happened. I was so worried about you, poor thing.'

'Ah, thanks. I just wanted to make sure you're okay after last night.'

'Me, sweetheart? I'm fine.' She pulled her pink cardigan tighter around her chest, clearly feeling the cold. She couldn't have been over 45 kilograms, and her skin was thin. Nevertheless, she dressed well every day, even though she often stayed inside. Her white perm was neatly done, matching the attention she gave to her neatly-pressed trousers and floral blouse.

'Did you have a fire in your place too?' he asked, as he peered inside her apartment. There was no evidence of any kind of disruption.

'Fire? Goodness, no,' she said. 'Are you feeling alright? Maybe you're still a little out of sorts after everything that happened. And your nose looks so swollen and sore! Why don't you come inside out of the cold, and have some tea?'

'No, thank you. Maybe another time. But the screaming – you must have heard something.'

'Oh, I did,' she replied, looking suddenly gloomy.

Will perked up a little. So he wasn't going mad. The screaming had been real. It'd happened. Although, he now wondered who was screaming, and what could've possibly happened to her.

'Yes, you gave quite a frightful yelp last night,' Mrs Simmons continued.

'Me?' asked Will, taken aback. 'What about the woman?'

'It was just you. I heard you scream. Only once, but it was loud. It sounded like you'd hurt yourself. I was going to come and check on you, but you stopped quickly, and I didn't want to be a bother after all you've been through. I know you're in a bad way – I thought you must've bumped yourself.'

Will didn't know what to say next. How could he have heard someone no one else could?

'Are you sure you're alright, Will? Come in and sit down.'

'No, I'm okay. Bye, Mrs Simmons.'

Back at his apartment, Will went into the bathroom. He stared at the sink, at the door, and at himself in the mirror. The fire had seemed so tangible, so terrifying. The screams had chilled him to the core, but his own neighbour hadn't seen or heard anything. The more he thought about it, the more real it seemed.

He grabbed his bottle of painkillers, and started thinking about other possibilities. Maybe he had a fever, or was experiencing a side effect from the medication. He took the bottle with him into the living room, and called Ravi.

The phone rang out and went to Ravi's message bank.

'Hey, it's Will. Sorry, I know you probably came off the night shift, but can you call me when you wake up? Thanks.'

Will sat down and massaged his temples. He was still tired, still sore, but he couldn't sleep, or even relax. He went to the kitchen to make himself a coffee.

While he was waiting for the kettle to boil, the intercom buzzed loudly, making him jump. His body was still on high alert, and he'd felt skittish all morning. Also, he rarely had visitors, and wasn't expecting anyone.

It was Detective Woods. Through the intercom, she said she wanted to speak with him about the case. After buzzing her in, he quickly shuffled about, attempting to tidy the living room. When he'd just finished scraping crumbs off the coffee table, she knocked on the door.

This time, Detective Woods was on her own. She greeted him with the same warm, attractive smile she'd given when they first met.

'Are you feeling any better?' she asked, examining his face.

'Definitely,' he lied, as he ushered Woods further into the apartment. They both sat at the small circular table by the kitchen.

'So, I've come with good news. We found all three of the people responsible for your attack. We'd been keeping a lookout for them, based on your description, and yesterday an officer picked one up. He was wearing the same hoodie you described, so it was an easy solve.'

'Oh, that's great,' Will replied. He truly hadn't expected such a quick result. In fact, he'd half-believed they wouldn't hold the kids to account.

'He had busted-up knuckles. It was obvious he'd just been in a fight. Anyway, the witness who helped you picked him out of a line-up, so we have substantial evidence.' Woods paused, and took a deep breath. 'Look, he's only a kid, but he's got a lengthy record. Hopefully, he'll stay in juvie for a while.'

Will nodded, attentive.

'With his record and how serious these charges are, he crumbled, cut a deal, and gave up the other two. We locked them both up this morning. They're at the station being processed as we speak, and I wanted to come over and tell you personally.'

'What about their parents? And did they say why they attacked me? I did nothing to them.' The pain and humiliation of being brutally attacked was one thing, but what bothered him most was why it'd happened.

'To be honest, when we spoke with their parents, they didn't seem to care about their kids, or what they'd done.'

Will shook his head, while Woods studied his reaction, frowning.

'Look, I get that you want to know why it happened, but they didn't give a reason. I tried, believe me, but I truly don't think there was any real reason for targeting you,' she said.

'Okay. Well, thanks for stopping by, I really appreciate it.'

Will lowered his eyes, and Woods sighed.

'Are you sure you're okay? I wasn't sure how you'd react, but I wanted you to know as soon as possible. That's it, there's nothing else to do now. Case closed.'

'Yeah, of course. I'm fine, really,' he said.

'If you're worried about them coming after you, don't be. I know it's easy for me to say, but I've spoken to them. They're nearly eighteen, so there's no way they'll do something stupid again – if they did, they'd be charged as adults.'

'That's good to hear… you know, because it happened just around the corner, so close to home.'

'I understand, and I'm glad to see you're on the mend. If you have any more questions, you have my card, and know where to find me. Don't forget the other card I gave you, either.'

'Sure, I won't. Thanks again, really.'

The news about the solved case was good, but Will still had other issues on his mind, and was desperate for Ravi to call him back. He needed to hear something comforting, like that hallucinations were a perfectly normal side effect of strong pain medication.

He spent the next hour pacing around his living room with his phone in hand. He wanted to keep ringing Ravi until he picked up, but knew he must've still been sleeping after his night shift. Will remained patient, until his phone finally rang. He answered it immediately.

'Hey, Ravi, sorry to bother you. I'm just feeling a little off, and I think it might be the pain meds.'

'You're on Panadeine Forte, right? Have you taken more than they told you?'

'No, I've followed the label exactly.'

'Well, how're you feeling?'

'A little strange, I suppose. Just tell me – what are the side effects?'

'It contains codeine,' Ravi said. 'So, occasional dizziness, confusion, fatigue, restlessness. There are some more severe side effects, but those are incredibly rare. We wouldn't be talking if you had them, you'd be right back in hospital. What's going on? Are you okay?'

'Yeah.' Will paused. 'I just had a terrible dream last night, that's all. I was having nightmares at the hospital too. Horrible dreams about bombs and explosions… so I thought the meds might cause that.'

He left out what he'd seen in his bathroom, which he was sure wasn't a dream. Until he processed it properly, he was afraid of the judgement he might receive.

Ravi softened his tone, going from doctor to friend.

'Will, it's been less than a week, and your body went through extreme stress. Have you spoken to a professional? I'd be happy to help you through it.'

'Thanks, but I think I'd like to keep this separate.'

'I get it, but you really should speak to someone.'

'The police gave me a victim support card.' Will moved toward the kitchen bench, searching for it in the stack of old mail and catalogues.

'Why don't you call them? While you're away from work, you need to look after yourself and get everything back on track.'

'Yeah, I will. Thanks, Ravi.'

'Anytime.'

Will hung up, and continued looking for the card. Maybe Ravi was right. He was under serious stress, and nothing like this had happened to him before. Perhaps he did just have a very realistic dream about a fire in his bathroom, and sleepwalked into the bathtub.

After fumbling through some more junk, he found the card and dialled the number.

'Hi,' Will said, when the call was answered on the first ring. 'Um, a police officer gave me your number after I got assaulted.'

'Oh, I'm sorry we have to meet this way – but we're here to look after each other! My name's Sarah, and I run the support group.'

Will liked Sarah's voice right away. She sounded warm and welcoming, putting him a little more at ease.

'It's good you called when you did, actually. We're gathering tonight, 7 p.m. at Pitt Street Uniting Church Hall. Why don't you come along? And what's your name, by the way?'

'Tonight?' Will was taken aback. He hadn't expected to be put on the spot so suddenly. 'Ah, I'm Will Denham. I guess I can be there.'

'No need to be nervous, Will. We're all just like you. You can just listen if you like, there's no obligation to contribute. But when our members talk openly about what happened to them, they tend to feel better. It's a safe place to share our experiences, and help one another out.'

'Sure, thank you. See you tonight.'

Will put his phone down with trembling hands, and took a long, deep breath.

SIX

Will arrived at Pitt Street Uniting Church a little before 7 p.m. The church itself was magnificent, but its small, detached hall looked sterile and plain compared to the main building. It was clearly much more modern, and was probably only built in the last few decades. Thick steel bars protected its windows, and a cinder block held its large door open, cheap fluorescent light flickering from the gap.

Will's stomach knotted at the thought of meeting an entire group of strangers, with his face still swollen, and being asked to tell his story. He took a deep breath, and walked into the hall.

The large room was almost completely empty. Will's rubber-soled shoes squeaked against the glossy floorboards. The only other occupant, a short woman with an auburn pixie cut and bright red cheeks, noticed his entry. She stood by a plastic trestle table folding pamphlets. Behind her, chairs were set up in a circle.

'Hi, I'm Sarah. You must be Will! Come on in,' she said, a big smile on her round face. Quickly, she finished sorting the pamphlets, and met Will with a firm handshake, before ushering him toward the table.

'Have a look at these. If you ever want to speak to a psychologist, there are plenty I could recommend, and all their information is here.'

Will started going through the colourful leaflets as Sarah kept talking.

'You've made a great first step. I expect a few more people here tonight. All we'll do is share whatever we want to share, so just relax and contribute as much as you want.'

'I probably won't talk much tonight. As I said on the phone, a police officer gave me your card, but I wasn't sure I'd even come.'

'Ah, yes. Aubrey Woods, I expect. She's a big advocate for us, and I know many people come here because of her.' Sarah made some final touches to her set-up and looked at Will sympathetically. 'What's important is that you're here now, and there's definitely no pressure to speak.'

'Thanks. You know Detective Woods, then?'

'Of course – she comes along to meetings when she can. Hopefully, you can hear her story someday. It's quite inspiring.'

'Her story? Something happened to her?'

'Yes.' Sarah pursed her lips and looked down. 'A few years back, she got hurt pretty badly responding to a work call.'

Will said nothing. Woods had been pretty serious about him calling the group, but he'd never thought she'd been a participant herself.

Sarah sat within the circle and invited him to join her. 'She has a dangerous job. I'm sure you'll have the chance to hear about it eventually, but it's for her to tell, not me.'

'How many people are you expecting tonight?' He'd begun counting the surrounding chairs, and was uncomfortable to see more than he'd anticipated.

'Usually, it's around a dozen, but sometimes as little as two or three. It doesn't matter to me, even if just one person comes. I'm just glad I can help someone. I actually used to be a psychologist, but now I'm a full-time single parent, so I run these meetings once a week. It's nice to still give something back.'

Will nodded. After an awkward moment of silence, several people entered the hall. There were three men and two women, ranging in age from around eighteen up to seventy. None of them resembled the weak-looking or broken-down stereotype of what Will had thought of as a victim. They all walked with confidence and familiarity, like old friends proud to be together. Sarah stood and greeted them, before introducing Will to each member. They were immediately receptive to the newcomer, paying no attention to his injuries and shaking hands to welcome him. Moments later, two more people entered the hall, both middle-aged, large-set men, still in high-visibility work clothing. After the second round of introductions and more warm welcomes for Will, the group sat down, and Sarah opened the meeting.

'Good evening, everyone. You've all met Will here. It's his first time with us, and you all remember how hard it is to make that first step toward healing, so please keep that in mind tonight.' Turning to Will, she spoke directly to him. 'So, we start by opening the floor to let people share what's on their mind. Maybe they'll talk about what happened to them, and how they managed the complex range of emotions they went through, or they'll simply discuss how they're feeling right now. There's no judgement – it's an open space to say whatever's on your mind.'

Will nodded and looked around the group, trying to pick who he thought would go first.

Sarah clapped her hands. 'Now, who'd like to start us off?'

An Asian man in a black leather jacket slowly raised his hand. He had spiky hair, and looked to be in his early twenties.

'Wonderful, thank you, Tim. Whenever you're ready.'

'Thanks,' Tim said, and cleared his throat. 'So, as I've said before, two robbers held me up at gunpoint when I was a bartender. I handed over money as they demanded, so they didn't hurt me, but I had to quit my job. I just couldn't go back there. I spent a lot of time thinking about that night, over and over, until I couldn't even leave the house. But after getting help – coming here, and seeing a psychiatrist – things have gotten much better for me. Yesterday, I had my first shift at a new pub. It's the first time I've worked since the robbery. I was pretty anxious, but it felt great taking that big step. My parents were worried too, but I want to open my own bar one day, so I couldn't just walk away from the industry. It's hard, and I still think about what happened, but my doctor said I've made great progress.'

The group clapped, and a few people close to Tim patted him on the back and shook his hand. He looked proud of himself. It was nice to see the support he received, and hear how he'd gotten himself back on track.

For the next thirty minutes, different people within the group spoke about being a victim of various crimes. Assault, armed robbery, stalking. The most striking story Will heard was from a middle-aged woman named Louise Hollis, who'd spent years in an extremely physically and sexually abusive relationship, until she killed her tormentor after a particularly nasty assault. She cried as she recounted the severe exhaustion she'd felt during the long and brutal trial. Ultimately, the jury had found her not guilty, because she'd acted in self-defence.

It was heartbreaking. Although many in the room had clearly heard it before, Will could've heard a pin drop as she recounted every painful detail. Although she'd escaped with her life, she did so by having to take another's. It was something Will could only imagine as being an act of pure and utter desperation.

When Louise finished, the group applauded her, and the mood lifted again. However, after listening to such a tragic story, Sarah announced it was time to have a break.

Everyone left their seats and stretched. A few stared at their phones, while others spoke with each other. Some tried to make small talk with Will, but he excused himself and walked to the side of the hall. As he gazed out a window, at the row of shops and office buildings across the street, he saw flames flickering wildly in the window of a shop.

Will took a second to process what he was seeing. Given his recent strange encounter with the bathroom fire, he took a little longer to convince himself it was real, before panic rushed through him.

'Fire!' he screamed. 'Over there, across the street!'

He ran to the end of the hall, and was out the door before anyone else reacted. As he sprinted out the side gate, he saw the small convenience store on the opposite side of the road now totally engulfed in fire.

The heat was overwhelming. The closer he got, the harder it was to breathe, and the more his skin ached. Unable to bear the intense light of the flames, he shielded his eyes. He wouldn't be able to get much closer.

Fumbling his phone out of his pocket, he wondered why nobody else was trying to clear the area. The street was quiet, but there were a few pedestrians walking about further down, and cars passing by without stopping. As he dialled the emergency number, two members of the support group, Brad and Jessica, ran up to his side.

Everything slowed. The licking flames became sluggish, and all Will could hear was Brad's voice as he whispered in his ear.

'It wasn't an accident.'

'What? Come on, we have to do something,' Will said desperately.

Jessica's breath brushed his neck as she leaned in too. 'Not now, but soon. Save her.'

'I need to call the fire brigade!'

Then, that same ear-piercing scream split the silence. It sounded like the same terrified woman, now much louder than she'd been the night before. Will cowered and covered his ears.

'Stop!' Brad took hold of Will's shoulders. 'There is no fire!'

'What are you talking about?' he asked, unable to understand why neither of them were helping.

'There's nothing there – look,' Jessica said, and pointed across the road.

Will raised his head.

The convenience store was perfectly intact. The screaming had stopped. Staring at the building, he lowered his hands, before he lost all stability in his legs and collapsed to the ground. Brad did his best to soften his fall, but was met with dead weight.

Will felt sick. He could still feel the sting of the fire on his skin. He'd smelt it, heard it, seen it. It had suffocated him. He couldn't understand what was happening.

'Come on, let's get you inside,' Brad said.

He and Jessica helped Will stand, and walked him back to the hall. Sarah was waiting just outside the door with a chair. Will flopped into it and looked up at Brad.

'You told me it wasn't an accident.' He turned to Jessica. 'Why did you tell me to save her? What did you mean?'

'What are you talking about?' Brad asked slowly, as he knelt down to his eye level. 'We didn't say any of that.'

Will's head was aching. It had been so real. The stench of smoke was still stuck in his nostrils.

'Just take some deep breaths and try to relax. I'm going to call an ambulance,' Sarah said, and took out her phone.

'No! I don't need an ambulance, I'm fine.'

'I don't think you are.' Sarah sighed. 'I've seen behaviour like this before, and I'm worried.'

'I'm going home. I'm just exhausted and stressed out, okay? I need to sleep. I'm sorry I caused trouble.' Will stood and strode toward the street.

Brad called, 'Will, please! Stop!'

Will didn't look back. As he made his way past the intact convenience store, he shuddered. Nothing made sense, but he was so sure about what he'd seen.

Back at his apartment, he closed the door behind him and sank to the floor. He rested his head in his hands, unable to believe he'd had what everyone at the church must've thought was a full-blown meltdown.

As he made his way to bed, Will felt a strong, raw instinct he couldn't explain. It told him that he wasn't ill, but that something strange was happening to him.

SEVEN

The next morning, Will got up with the sun. While he stood in the kitchen picking at his breakfast, he examined his bandaged ribs and shoulder. They were mending nicely, but still swollen, and a little tender.

Whatever was going on in his head, he wouldn't keep taking the pain medication. Maybe if he lived as he did before the assault, everything would go back to normal.

After breakfast, Will took a shower to completely wake himself up. He stood under the warm water and let it soothe his stiff body. As he rinsed his hair, a sharp sensation crawled up his shoulders. He jumped out of the water. Steam was building in the shower, and the water was piping hot. Cursing the old plumbing, he adjusted the knobs to cool the water down.

The temperature continued to rise. Will reached for a towel to wrap around his hands, so he could reach through the scalding water and turn it off. The steam grew unbearably hot, and so dense that he could no longer see the taps, flickering bright red as it filled the bathroom.

Will pulled his hand back. As he watched the water and red steam transform to bright flames, an unusual feeling of safety swept over him. The heat in the bathroom grew more intense, but he knew he wouldn't be harmed. When the piercing screams returned, instead of cowering and covering his ears, he stood perfectly still.

His eyes snapped shut. Opening them again, he found himself

inside an unfamiliar building. It was collapsing around him as a fire roared through it. Flames wrapped around his body, and although he felt no pain, the fire was hot, and his skin warmed and tingled. Smoke entered his lungs. As the fire rose, he fell to his knees, coughing and spitting. Rafters fell, wood crackling. Will stayed low, covering his head as he moved through the flames. They ripped the building down around him while he struggled to breathe, doing his best to find an exit through the thick smoke. Before he could, his eyes snapped shut again. Just as quickly as he'd entered the fire, he was gone.

Now, he was on the deserted street outside the burning building. It was double-storey, with a shop on the ground level, and an office or small residence above. A sign on the lower floor read Tony's Convenience. Flames swallowed the sign, and it fell to the ground, shattering to pieces.

A man stood in the middle of the road. He was facing away from Will, and carrying a large red petrol can. He was short, stocky, and completely bald, and a thick scar ran up the back of his left forearm. Without looking back, he walked away, until he disappeared from sight.

The flames climbed higher, lashing the building with tremendous raw power. A scream came from the top floor of the building. Will recognised it immediately as the same scream he'd become familiar with. Looking up to the second floor, he saw that one of the street-facing windows was now open, the shadow of a person's upper body sticking out. He tried to focus on the body, but couldn't make out a face or any features. The high-pitched scream continued, begging for help.

Will was paralysed. He couldn't speak or move. All he could do was stand and watch the building burn, trapping the person on the upper floor. Just before the fire reached their silhouette, a cool breeze brushed the back of Will's neck.

The window was empty. Flames continued to consume the building. The breeze continued to flick at his neck, and slowly, he turned around.

The screaming woman was inches from his face. Her frail arms were covered in welts, the burnt skin on her face barely holding on to her bones.

Will gasped, lightheaded. The woman lifted one of her blackened arms, and just as she was about to touch his face, his eyes forced themselves open.

He was back in his bathroom. The shower was running normally. He snatched at the taps to turn them off and sat on the bathroom floor, panting and trembling.

Wiping the sweat from his face, he tried to catch his breath. He remembered everything he'd seen in vivid detail. The burning shop, the man holding the red petrol can, the piercing screams from the top floor. Was it connected to everything he'd experienced in the last couple of days? He didn't know who the woman was, but her pained howling still rang in his ears.

His mind raced as he stood by the sink and splashed cool water on his face. There must've been a reason for what he'd seen. A message, perhaps. Had this actually happened? Or was it about to?

He recalled the sign stuck to the building. Running to his living room, he switched on the computer and searched for Tony's Convenience. The first result told him the store was currently open, and located just off Cleveland Street at Surry Hills, about a ten-minute walk from his place. He clicked on the street-view map. The shopfront was exactly as he'd seen it earlier. It even had the same sign on the wall. He continued searching for information about any fires at the shop, but there was nothing.

Still, what he'd seen must've meant something. He'd never even heard of Tony's Convenience until today – how could he see something he hadn't even known existed?

For the next few hours, he kept researching fires in Surry Hills. There'd been plenty. Several homes had been destroyed over the years, and many had received local media attention. As tragic as they all were, there was nothing close to what he'd seen.

Turning the computer off, he stomped into the living room and threw himself onto the couch. The 11 a.m. news update was just starting. A scrolling banner read, Breaking News: Fire in Sydney. Will sat bolt upright and turned the volume up.

The news anchor began, 'In Surry Hills, Sydney, fire has torn through a local shop and the residence upstairs. Emergency crews have arrived, but at least one person is believed to be dead. We'll now go to reporter John Nelson, who is on the scene.'

The screen flashed to a smouldering building. Immediately, Will knew it was the same building he'd seen only hours earlier. He sat frozen, watching firefighters battle the blaze. A reporter with slick hair and a fitted suit appeared in front of the camera.

'Behind me stood Tony's Convenience, a popular store here in the community, which had been operating for almost forty years. It's now completely destroyed, as a fire raged through the building earlier today. Tragically, firefighters have recovered the body of an elderly woman who was living above the shop. The fire is under control, but is believed to be suspicious. Firefighters and police will remain here for some time.'

Will sat staring at the TV, winded. There was so much to process. The flames, the screaming, the whispers in his ear. Had it all led up to this fire? It couldn't be a coincidence. The words Jessica hissed the night before, 'Save her,' played over and over in his mind.

Guilt washed over him. He'd refused to trust himself, and now someone was dead, a building destroyed. It was over. His chance to do something was gone. All because he'd been battling with his own mind, continuing to deny it meant something real.

Will walked himself again through all he'd seen. The news mirrored everything, except for the man with the scar on his arm.

Suddenly, he saw the missing gap. The fire was deliberately lit. It must've been him – the man with the red petrol can.

He reached for his phone, dialled 000, and requested the police. The call connected, and the female operator asked for his emergency.

Will cleared his throat. 'Um, I saw on the news there was a fire at Surry Hills. Tony's Convenience. I think it was lit deliberately, and just wanted to make sure you knew that.'

'Okay, sir,' she said. 'Did you see something that could help the police?'

Stuttering, Will slapped his forehead. He hadn't rehearsed this call, but still should've expected an obvious question like that.

'Sir, are you there?'

'Ah, yeah.'

He still didn't know how to answer her question. The operator broke the silence first.

'What's your name and address? We'll record your information, and pass it to the police. They can talk directly with you.'

Will's heart jumped. Hanging up the phone, he cursed himself again.

How could he ever explain what he saw?

NINE

'Hey, I need to talk to you about something, and it's going to sound really weird.'

Unsure what to do after hanging up on the police, Will had called Ravi. On the other end of the phone, Ravi paused.

'Okay, I'm listening.'

'So, you know when we spoke the other day, and I asked about my pain meds? Then I said I was having bad dreams?'

'Yeah,' Ravi replied slowly.

'They weren't just dreams. I was seeing something that hadn't happened yet. Like a vision.'

'What are you talking about?' Ravi replied, disbelief clear in his voice.

'The fire that happened today, where the lady died. Did you hear about it?'

'Yeah, it was on the news.'

'I saw it happen before it did. For days now, I've been seeing that fire.'

'Okay, hilarious, I get it. I guess you're pretty bored stuck at home. Listen, I'm getting ready for work, I better go.'

'Listen to me!' It was the first time Will had ever raised his voice at Ravi. He didn't reply, and Will continued, his temper increasing. 'I know what I saw. I know it sounds crazy, but I'm not making it up. Before I spoke to you the other day, my entire bathroom caught fire right in front of me, but it all happened in my head.'

Pausing, Will tried to gather himself. He didn't want to yell, and in any case, he hadn't expected to be believed right away. After all, Ravi was the most rational person Will knew. To him, the idea of visions would be either preposterous or easily explained with a medical diagnosis.

'Okay, Will. I'll be at work in half an hour. Come and stop by, and let's talk about this. Face to face.'

'Yeah, alright. I'll see you soon.'

Will jabbed hard at the end call button and slammed his phone down. Would anyone ever believe him?

While he waited for Ravi to get to the hospital, he read articles about the fire at Tony's Convenience. It never took journalists long to start doing background research. One article identified the elderly woman who'd died in the fire – Beverly Lawson, 78 years old. She'd lived in the unit above the shop for the past four years, ever since the death of her husband. There was a quote from a neighbour saying what a lovely and kind person she was, and how she'd be sorely missed. It only exacerbated the guilt Will was feeling. A person had lost her life, and he could've done something to save her.

***

During his rounds, Ravi continually checked his phone for messages from Will. He'd dedicated his career to diagnosing and treating all sorts of mental health disorders, and after speaking with Will – coupled with his recent trauma – Ravi was truly concerned about him. When a text finally came through, Ravi immediately dropped everything he was doing and went to meet Will.

Ravi pushed through the heavy plastic doors leading to the

loading dock and waste disposal facilities. The area was empty, aside from Will standing nervously behind a dumpster, shuffling his weight back and forth. It had only been a few days since Ravi last saw him, but he looked like he hadn't slept since. His hair was a mess, his t-shirt sweat-stained. He looked up at Ravi, held his ground, and didn't speak.

Ravi placed his hands on Will's shoulders, examining his still-bruised face and tired, bloodshot eyes.

'You don't look too good.'

Will ignored him. 'I don't want anyone around the hospital to know I'm here, alright? About what I said before – I'm completely serious. I had a vision, saw all these signs that a fire was going to happen, and then it did. Don't you get it?'

Ravi released his gentle grip.

'Come on, now. That's not possible.'

'I know what I saw, Ravi!'

Ravi rubbed his chin. Normally, he could be rational when dealing with his patients, but this was affecting him a little more personally. He sighed to himself when he decided what he needed to do.

'We need to have a proper chat. Why don't you come inside?'

'I know what you're trying to do. I'm not sick, and I won't be one of your patients.'

Ravi attempted to take Will by the arm. Will snatched himself away and took a step back.

'Think about it,' Will said. 'My head got hit pretty hard, right? I had a concussion, and all those headaches.'

'Yes,' Ravi said softly, as he looked over his shoulder. They were still alone in the loading dock.

'I think something happened when I got knocked around. That's when this all started. It must have triggered something.'

Will was sounding more and more desperate, and Ravi's concerns were growing. He must've truly convinced himself of the strange delusion he was having.

'What you went through was awful, and you're still recovering, but no one can see the future.'

'You have to trust me! I also saw a short, bald man with a scar on his arm, carrying a red petrol can. He's the one who started the fire at the shop, and the police don't know yet. I already let someone die – he can't get away with it. But if you don't believe me, how will the police?'

'Will, you need to come inside. Talk to someone properly, before this gets out of control.'

Will grabbed Ravi by his shirt, driving him back into the metal dumpster. The clang of his impact rang through the whole loading dock, but was quickly drowned out by Will's shouting.

'I don't know why this is happening to me, but it is! I've never been so sure of anything in my life. Ravi, I could feel it like I was there. Fire on my skin, smoke in my lungs. And now what? You're treating me like one of your mental patients?'

Ravi remained frozen, panting under Will's firm grip.

Will was unpredictable. He'd never shown an ounce of aggressiveness before, and Ravi was frightened.

'If you won't help me, I'll just figure this out myself,' Will said, and released Ravi.

As he watched Will walk away, Ravi caught his breath, but found that he was still shaking. His friend was acting way out of character. Without a proper assessment, he didn't know exactly what was happening to Will, but he was worried. Seeing things was never a good sign, and could be a symptom of many serious disorders.

Ravi wished he could've helped Will in an easier way, but urgent measures needed to be taken. He needed to call the police before

Will had a delusional episode, and hurt himself or someone else.

***

Will walked with long, fast strides, struggling to vent his rage. He regretted lashing out. All of his frustrations had brought him to the boiling point, but he still planned on apologising to Ravi once the dust settled. For now, he charged on, headed for the Surry Hills Police Station. Regardless of whether they believed him, he was going to tell the police what he'd seen.

He had nothing to lose anymore. He owed it to Beverly Lawson to help catch the person responsible for her death, which he now knew he'd been given every opportunity to prevent.

Hurrying through the police station's automatic glass doors, Will felt the cool breeze from the air conditioner calm his heated face a little. Without hesitation, he charged toward the front counter, where a uniformed constable sat typing on a computer.

Will cleared his throat. 'I have some information about the fire at Tony's Convenience,' he said, with as much confidence as he could.

The constable glanced up, stared at Will, then down at his screen. Will tapped his hands on the counter. The constable looked back to him, scratching his short, dark beard.

'What's your name, sir?'

'Will Denham.'

'Come with me, please.' He stood up from the desk.

Will was ushered into a small interview room at the front of the station. Another constable with a tall, thick frame was called in to stay with him, and stood still with his arms folded while the first left the room. A moment later, he returned and sat in front of Will.

'We've had a call from City South Hospital about you. They've asked us to get you back there for an assessment. I've called an ambulance, and it's on its way.'

Will's fists tightened.

'I don't need the hospital!' he shouted, shooting to his feet. The officers took him by the arm and sat him back down. He cursed Ravi under his breath.

'You need to stay still,' the bearded constable said sternly. 'I don't want to handcuff you, but I will if I have to.'

'You don't understand! I'm not crazy, I just need to talk to someone about the fire.'

The officers looked at each other and raised their eyebrows. There was a loud knock on the door, and before either officer could stand, it opened from the outside. Detective Aubrey Woods entered the room and gave Will a sympathetic look.

'Hi, Will.'

'Detective, thank God,' he said. 'Tell these guys I don't need to go to the hospital.'

'Could you give us a second?' Woods asked the two officers. They gave her quizzical looks, and she nodded. After they left the room, she turned to Will.

'I heard that you were here,' she said, removing her dark blazer and draping it over a chair.

'I wanted to give some information about the fire at Tony's Convenience.'

'Some people are pretty worried about you. Are you okay, Will?'

'It's all just a huge misunderstanding.'

'Before I heard the hospital was looking for you, I was actually going to stop by your place to chat about the fire,' she said, as she took a seat opposite him and folded her arms. 'You see, as part of the investigation, I reviewed the emergency calls we received about the fire. Most were just people calling for the fire brigade, but then I saw a call from your number. The recording was unusual. Do you want to tell me what that was all about?'

Will looked at Detective Woods for a while. There wouldn't be an easy way to tell her what he'd seen, so he decided to just come out with it.

'I promise you, every word of what I'm going to say is true.' Will took a slow, deep breath and tried to compose himself. Detective Woods stared directly at him, and didn't say a word.

'I had visions,' he declared, not breaking eye contact. 'I knew there was going to be a fire. I saw it for two days. It started off really cryptic and strange, with fires appearing in weird places, and then I saw the burning building.'

Detective Woods exhaled, with an almost disappointed look on her face.

'Look, I know you've had a tough time lately, but we're all very busy here, and can't waste any time on lies, or prank emergency calls,' she said.

'I'm not lying, I swear!' Will said, shifting to the edge of his chair.

Woods kept her tone soft. 'We've already checked CCTV nearby, and I looked into your phone records and cell tower information. I know you weren't there. You weren't a witness, were you?'

'No, I'm telling you, I saw it in my head.'

'I think the hospital's right in wanting you to get checked out. What you're saying is pretty concerning, Will,' Woods said, standing.

Just before she left the room, Will called out after her.

'I know who lit the fire! He's a short, bald guy with a big scar down his arm.'

Woods stopped and looked at Will suspiciously.

'Who have you been speaking to? Another detective here?'

'I haven't spoken to anyone, but it's true, isn't it? You know who he is. He's bald and short, isn't he?' Will asked. Surely, Woods would have to believe him now.

'If his identity's been leaked, that could be really dangerous. My team's on the way to arrest him now.' Woods sat back down and frowned at Will. 'Who've you spoken to? My officers could be in trouble if he knows they're coming.'

'I swear, I didn't talk to anyone. I had a vision of him.'

With a deep and hostile glare, she got up and left the room. She returned minutes later. 'You're lucky. They've arrested the man responsible without any issues.'

'Detective, I promise no one said anything to me. But it's him, isn't it, with the scar down his arm?'

'Yes... that's correct.' Woods stared at Will.

'I'm glad you got him,' Will said, with a smile. 'So, who is he?'

She continued to study Will suspiciously. 'He was the owner of the store. It was pretty simple, really. He was losing a lot of money, so he took out a large insurance policy about six weeks ago and burnt the place down. It wasn't a very sophisticated crime.'

'The poor woman upstairs.' As Will remembered the sound of her screams, guilt washed over him again.

'Yes, it's tragic. Apparently, he didn't think she was home,' she said. 'Now, seriously, I don't know how you knew all this, but an information leak from this office is a serious matter. I will find out what's going on.'

'I told you, it happened in my head. Please believe me.'

Woods glanced out the small window.

'The ambulance is here. They'll take you to get some help.'

'I don't need help,' he begged. 'You heard everything I said – I knew about the guy with the scar. Tell them!'

'Considering all this talk of visions, I think you need to go.'

With that, she left the room.

TEN

Will spent the ride to the hospital in complete silence. He was cooperating because there was no point in giving the paramedics, who were simply doing their job, a hard time.

But he was angry. He'd trusted Ravi, and the favour hadn't been returned. What would the doctors do to him? Had Ravi told them what he'd said in confidence? If so, they too wouldn't believe him. Maybe they'd force-feed him drugs to keep him quiet and under control, to make him forget he'd ever had visions to begin with.

As the ambulance approached the hospital, Will devised a plan to get out of there as quickly as he could. He would act normal and calm, insist that there'd been some mistake, and deny having visions or telling Ravi anything of the kind. Then, when they were forced to apologise and release him, he'd promise not to sue.

The ambulance drove into the dock near the emergency department. Ravi was waiting for him, along with a nurse. As soon as the back doors opened, Ravi climbed inside.

'I'm sorry it had to come to this, I really am,' he said.

Will kept his eyes fixed on the roof of the ambulance.

While the paramedics helped him inside, he prepared to start his denial of any visions. However, he was ushered straight past triage. Ravi must've admitted him before he arrived, preventing him from pleading his case to the triage nurse.

He was escorted to a small, private room just outside the

psychiatric ward. The walls were pale blue, and featured landscape photographs in cheap frames. There were no windows, and the only furniture was two soft chairs.

When Ravi entered the room, Will sat with his arms folded, examining the photographs.

'Will, I hope you understand that I didn't want to do this,' Ravi said, as he took the chair opposite him. 'But we need to talk, so I can try to help you.'

'I don't need help,' grunted Will, still avoiding eye contact.

Ravi sighed and dragged his seat a little closer.

'I want to give you answers about why you're seeing and hearing all these things. Isn't that what you want?'

The pair sat in silence for five full minutes.

'Okay,' Ravi said, finally. 'You're going to have to stay here for a while. We'll talk soon, alright?'

The psychiatric unit looked much the same as any other hospital ward, with one difference: heavy-duty lockable doors. As two orderlies walked Will to the entrance of the ward, they were required to press a buzzer on the outer door, before identifying themselves to an intercom. The door clicked open shortly after. Will had been in this ward many times during his routine maintenance duties, and knew the only way out was for a security guard behind a secure Perspex screen to release the locks.

The only items in Will's assigned room were a thin bed and a TV bolted to the wall. He was given a heavily-starched hospital gown, and having worn the same outfit earlier in the week, he wasn't excited to get back into it. But he had little choice. After handing his old clothes to the orderly, he settled into the bed and mindlessly watched TV.

A couple of hours later, Will heard a light knock on his door. Slowly, it opened, and Ravi entered. He leaned against the wall, waiting, until Will broke the silence.

'Do you have any idea how humiliating it is to be brought here? Where everyone knows me, and now thinks I'm crazy?'

'I admitted you for PTSD, Will. The things you told me have stayed between us. People are just worried you're having a hard time after the assault.'

Will was relieved nobody knew the real reason he'd been brought into this ward, but it also ruined his chances of coming up with an elaborate denial. To get released as soon as possible, he'd have to focus on somehow convincing Ravi he was sane.

'I've apologised for the way things played out,' Ravi continued, 'but I won't apologise for trying to help you.'

'Why can't you just accept that it isn't so simple? I'm not sick. I spoke with the cops, and described the guy they arrested for the fire! How do you explain that? Ask them, they'll tell you!'

'I want to get started soon, so I'll come back later. We can go through everything, right from the start.'

Will ignored him, and went back to watching the TV. He wasn't looking forward to describing visions he knew were real, and having a doctor interpret them as something else to come up with a rubbish diagnosis. He decided his plan would be the same. Deny any visions, and say he made it all up, so not even Ravi could keep him in hospital.

He remained in bed for the rest of the afternoon. At 6 p.m., the news started. The opening story was about the arrest made in connection with the fire at Tony's Convenience. Will bolted upright and turned up the volume.

The same reporter who'd covered the fire during the 11.a.m news, wearing a navy suit with slick dark hair, continued with the story.

'Earlier in the day, we reported that Tony's Convenience at Surry Hills was burnt down, and an elderly resident in the upstairs apartment lost her life. Upon investigating the scene, police believed the fire was deliberately lit and began searching for a suspect. Earlier today, they arrested Tony Hartley, the long-time owner of the local store.'

As the camera showed earlier scenes of the shop in flames, Will fumbled for the emergency call button. Seconds later, a nurse came running in. Before she could say anything, he yelled, 'Get Doctor Sandeep, now!'

The nurse fled the room. When Ravi hurried in, Will pointed to the TV.

'Look at this!' he shouted.

On screen, the reporter said, 'Behind me is the home of Tony Hartley, who was taken into custody a short time ago. Police have remained on scene, searching the house for further clues as to the cause of the tragedy. It appears to have been financially motivated, as a large insurance policy was taken out weeks before Mr Hartley allegedly lit the fire.'

A photo of Tony Hartley flashed onscreen. Ravi looked back at Will, but didn't speak.

The scene returned to Hartley's residence, where police were leaving the house with several evidence bags. The camera panned to a detective who was carrying a large red petrol can.

'Detectives have seized several items believed to have been used in the offence,' the reporter said.

'See! I told you. The red can, the bald guy. I even picked his scar!' Will knew he had his proof, and Ravi couldn't deny it.

Ravi stared at Will.

'Say something,' Will demanded.

'I don't understand,' Ravi said.

'You saw it! The red petrol can – explain that.'

Ravi took off his glasses and scratched his head.

'I'm a doctor, Will. I don't know what that was, and I don't know what to tell you, but supernatural visions just can't happen.'

'Why not? Because your textbooks say they can't? You heard me describe Tony Hartley and the petrol can this morning, before he was even arrested.' Will got out of bed and pointed at the TV. 'Now you know I saw it.'

Ravi went to the door and closed it softly. He walked back to the bed and sat on the end, while Will remained standing.

'I just… it just doesn't make any sense.'

'I know it sounds crazy,' Will said, more gently. 'Believe me, I get it. When I first started seeing things, I didn't know what was happening. That's why I came to you – to work it out, not get locked up.'

'I'm sorry, I really am. Everything you were saying was consistent with schizophrenia, and I panicked. I still don't even know what to say.'

'I can't explain it either, but I need you to believe me.'

Ravi let out a deep exhale.

'I do. I mean, I can't argue with you, after what I just saw. Still, this just seems impossible. It's… all very confusing.'

'You're telling me.'

Will sat back down upon the bed, finally able to relax a little.

'I'm sorry it got heated this morning,' he said. 'You know that's not like me.'

'Don't worry about it.'

'So, what now?'

'Tell me what you've seen. I'm curious about what it was like.'

Will had expected Ravi would ask him this, but as part of a mental health assessment, without believing the visions occurred. Now, he genuinely wanted to know.

'Well, it first happened in my bathroom when I got home from the hospital. I woke up sweating, and then – this is going to sound weird—'

'Hey,' Ravi interrupted. 'It's already weird, but I'm listening.'

Will nodded. 'My bathroom caught on fire. It seemed so real… I could feel the heat, and the flames consumed the room, but it didn't harm me. The second time, I saw a building on the street go up in flames. It wasn't until the third that I actually saw the shop, the woman, all burnt. Then I noticed Tony, and could kind of piece it all together. But I still didn't understand it. I couldn't tell if I was dreaming or awake.'

Will looked down and picked at his fingernails. 'The next time I see something like that, I won't wait around for something bad to follow.'

'Will it happen again, though?'

He hadn't considered that. He'd been so busy dealing with the visions of the fire that he'd just assumed he'd have more.

'My concussion – could it have had anything to do with this?'

'There's no science to back me up here, but maybe,' Ravi said. 'You'd never had them before, so it's a reasonable assumption. Before you go, I could do an MRI, to check if anything's different.'

'Sure.'

Will thought a scan might provide some answers. Besides, things were good again between him and Ravi, so he trusted him with the results.

Later that evening, after Ravi signed him out of the psych ward, they went downstairs to where the MRI would be performed. Lying on the sliding bed, Will tried to remain as still as he could, and ignore the loud humming, bright lights, along with his own apprehensive thoughts. What if his visions were a side effect of something serious, like a tumour or brain infection?

When the scan was done, Ravi walked in with the results.

'Clear,' he said. 'Everything looks perfectly normal.'

Will didn't know whether to be happy or not. A clear scan couldn't be bad, but he still didn't have any answers.

'I'd love to get you scanned during one of your visions,' Ravi whispered to Will.

'If I could control them, so would I,' Will whispered back.

Ravi discharged Will immediately after the MRI. As he left the hospital, a few of his colleagues stopped to wish him well, with some telling him how brave he was. News and gossip travelled fast, so Will truly appreciated that no one knew the actual reason he was brought in.

He flagged down a taxi to take him home. It was dark, and he still wasn't ready to make the night-time walk. When he returned to his apartment, Rosie called him with an invitation to visit her and the family for the weekend, which he accepted. It was just what he needed – to get away from the city, see his niece, and have a bit of quiet time.

ELEVEN

As the night grew darker and quieter, Don Evans and Chris Pollard sat patiently in their heavily-tinted black BMW, a car unlawfully acquired by Pollard only hours before. The lights were still on inside their target – a large ivy-wrapped townhouse in Sydney's inner south-east.

Evans and Pollard met three weeks prior through a mutual friend. Although the plan involved their complete cooperation, they were unsure if they trusted each other yet, and watched the house in complete silence.

Evans had planned the entire operation and knew it couldn't possibly fail. He would've preferred to complete the task alone, but it required a bit of muscle, which was why he'd recruited his partner in crime.

Pollard was his polar opposite. While Evans resembled a well-groomed car salesman in both dress and appearance, Pollard was heavily tattooed, with the face of a well-seasoned boxer.

Finally, Evans broke the quiet.

'What's with the crucifix?' he asked, looking at the large cross tattooed on Pollard's right bicep. Evans was dressed in dark jeans and a long-sleeved shirt, but Pollard wore a tight white singlet, his bulky shoulders and arms on full display.

'I'm Catholic,' Pollard replied, as though it was a stupid question.

'Yes, and I'm sure you're an upstanding member of the Church, but I don't want anyone noticing specifics.' Evans ran his fingers through his slick black hair, before reaching into a bag for a dark hoodie and a pair of leather gloves. 'Put these on.'

Just as Evans had predicted, about five minutes past 11 p.m., the house lights went off. The pair waited in silence.

An hour later, the entire street had shut down for the night. It was poorly lit, lined with tall, thick trees that hid the bright glow of the streetlights. Evans and Pollard put on their leather gloves and pulled balaclavas over their faces, before hurrying toward the Sullivan residence. Pollard went first, using the ivy's wood lattice support to climb the side of the house, with Evans following. They both made it to the balcony easily enough.

The sliding door to the master bedroom felt loose beneath Pollard's hands. He applied firm pressure and lifted it, shifting it across to make a space large enough to fit through. The room was dark, but they had enough light from the open door to navigate their way around.

Pollard strode to the bed and punched the man sleeping on the left, before forcing a hand over his mouth and pulling him to the floor. Martin Sullivan was a large man, and proved to be a slight challenge, but the element of surprise went in Pollard's favour. The struggle woke Martin's wife, Abby, who sat up quickly.

Evans was waiting. He put her in a chokehold from behind and delivered an injection straight into her neck. Abby was petite, barely five feet tall, and looked even smaller in pink flannel pyjamas. After a few seconds of struggling, she was unconscious.

Evans let her flop back onto the sheets. Pollard was even more efficient than he'd hoped – Martin was already hogtied and gagged. With two more hard punches, he was unconscious. Evans left a note on the bed, then the two carried Abby down the stairs, out the front door, and into their car.

In and out in under five minutes. Just as Evans had planned.

***

Shortly after, Martin Sullivan regained consciousness. Whimpering through the gag, he tried to untie himself quietly, unsure whether his attackers were still in the house.

He eventually wriggled out of the ropes. Standing up, he looked around the room, but couldn't find Abby. He tore through the house, shouting her name, heedless of the intruders. When he realised she wasn't there, he fell to the ground and wept, trying not to imagine what must've happened to her.

Minutes later, Martin pulled himself together. He limped upstairs and found his phone on the bedside table. As he unlocked it, he saw a folded piece of paper lying on the pillow.

Mr Sullivan,

If you are reading this, congratulations on being conscious. If we wanted you dead, you would be, but you are far too important to us.

We have Abby. Don't worry; if you do as we say, she won't be hurt. She is merely our security in the investment of robbing you.

You will pay us $1,000,000 in Bitcoin. Don't play dumb about your experience with cryptocurrency. We know exactly who you are. We know everything about you.

From my analysis of the market, I expect Bitcoin will hit a low of $35,000 by 8 p.m. on Saturday. At that exchange rate, we will expect no less than 28.572 Bitcoin from you. Two days will give you plenty of time to consider your options, but I assure you, there is only one. If you fail to transfer the funds, she will be killed.

Call the police if you want. In fact, I encourage it. I have no concerns. They will not catch me.

Stay by your phone for further instructions. I will call after 8 p.m. on Friday night.

Martin read the note twice more. It was written with no emotion. Written as if it was a business trade – Bitcoin for the life of his wife. The author's confidence was sickening, but after how quickly and brutally they'd subdued him, he did not for one second believe they were bluffing.

What also frightened him was their knowledge of him and his wife. They were clearly aware of his background in cryptocurrency.

Feeling sick, he did what the note said and called the police.

***

Within minutes, uniformed officers from Surry Hills Station arrived at the Sullivan residence, followed by the night shift detectives, Woods and Lapis.

Martin was waiting on the street, wearing a dressing gown stained with blood from his cut lip. After escorting him back inside, Lapis photographed the note and sealed it in an evidence bag. Woods offered some brief sympathy to the distraught Martin, but wasted no time in getting as much information from him as possible. While her theoretical training in kidnapping cases told her to keep things quiet, it appeared the offenders expected police involvement, so she took it as an opportunity to search for witnesses. She called over the uniformed officers.

'I want two of you to canvass this side of the road, and two on the other,' she said. 'I don't care if people are asleep – keep banging on the doors until you wake them. Someone around here must have CCTV, or have at least heard something. Still, don't give them much information. Go.'

The officers broke into teams.

'You think this is legit?' Lapis asked Woods. 'I mean, how often do you hear of a kidnapping for ransom?'

'We treat it like it is until proven otherwise,' she replied. 'This guy's petrified. Something nasty happened here for sure.'

'I want to have a good look through the house, see if anything was left behind.'

'You go. I'll stay with Sullivan.'

Thirty minutes later, Detective Sergeants Ian Yule and Rodney O'Donnell from the Robbery and Serious Crime Squad arrived on the scene. Both were gruff, well-built men in their mid-50s wearing jeans and dark polo shirts. As they walked toward the Sullivan residence, Yule wrapped his police ID lanyard around his neck and patted down his thick black beard, while O'Donnell busied himself with his phone. Woods and Lapis met them in the front yard, and got them up to speed.

'Home invasion and kidnapping,' Woods began. 'Abby Sullivan, thirty-three years old and the wife of Martin Sullivan, thirty-five, is missing. There was a ransom note left behind.'

'Yes, we heard about that – the million in Bitcoin, and the taunt about calling the police. Very unusual. Can I see it?' Yule asked.

'I've bagged it up, but here's a photo.' Lapis took out his phone, and the sergeants read the note in silence.

'Go on,' Yule said, when they'd finished.

Woods continued. 'Two unknown males broke in, both wearing balaclavas. The victim woke up to being dragged out of bed by the bigger of the two. During the assault, he saw the other wrestling with his wife, who'd woken up by that stage. Neither of them said a single word. He was gagged and tied, then knocked out, and woke a little while ago to find the note.'

'The note's a worry,' O'Donnell said. 'It's very confident, but it's possible that confidence might hurt them too. Seems like they know Sullivan, or at least his routine. Has he offered any suspects?'

'We haven't got that far yet. He's pretty shaken up,' Woods

replied. 'Apparently, he was involved in some huge American cryptocurrency deal, which got a bit of media attention in the digital finance world. I'd never heard of him, though.'

'Me neither, but it might give us another lead,' Yule said. 'Okay, we'll get set up and have a chat with him soon. Could you two stay on for a while? Our team will run the investigation, but we could use all the help we can get.'

As Woods nodded, she saw the uniformed team making their way back to the house.

'We couldn't find any witnesses, sorry,' the senior officer reported. 'No one heard a thing, and none of the houses have CCTV.'

'Okay, thanks,' she said. 'You guys can get out of here. We'll call if we need anything else.'

Yule watched them leave, tilting his head back in thought. 'So, we have no footage, no witnesses aside from Martin, and no one even heard anything.'

'What do we do now?' Woods asked.

'We run forensics and wait for the kidnappers to call. Hopefully, a trace on Martin's phone can tell us where they are,' Yule said. 'But otherwise, we wait.'

TWELVE

It was a clear day in Queanbeyan. It always felt a little colder than Sydney, but the air was fresh, and the streets were peaceful. As Rosie drove him away from the train station, Will wondered if he'd leave the city someday to be a little closer to his family.

When they pulled into Rosie's driveway, Will could see Claire waiting on the front porch. She was sitting patiently with a large blonde doll in her lap. The moment Will got out of the car, she ran full-speed directly at him.

'Uncle Will!' she screamed, as she crashed into his legs. Will picked her up and kissed her on the cheek. She'd grown considerably since he last saw her, and resembled her mother, with a long, thin body and dark hair tied in a ponytail.

'Wow, you're so heavy now!' he said.

'Claire, be gentle,' Rosie warned. 'Remember what I said about Uncle Will being sore?'

'Oh, I'm fine.' Even as Will said it, he realised Claire was the most weight he'd held in a week, and his cracked ribs did not appreciate it. He put her back down when he couldn't tolerate her weight any longer.

Claire giggled.

'Your nose looks funny,' she said, and crinkled her face up.

'It sure does,' Will replied, as happily as he could. 'But it'll go back to normal soon.'

'Come on, let's get inside,' Rosie said.

Her house was single-storey and newly-developed. It had all the space they could want, and Claire seemed happy filling the large backyard with all sorts of toys.

Ben came to greet Will straight away. He was a tall, fit man, with strong shoulders and a kind, welcoming smile. Will had always liked him – he was good to Rosie, and had really supported the family when they'd lost their mother years earlier.

'I'm so glad you're here, it's been way too long,' Ben said, as he shook Will's hand. 'Make yourself at home. Claire wanted you to sleep in her room, but we figured you'd prefer to be in a room of your own.'

'I left a doll in there for you, though. In case you need it,' Claire said.

'How thoughtful, thank you,' Will replied, with a chuckle.

After the four of them ate an early lunch, Claire decided she wanted to show Will the park around the corner, so Rosie, Will and Claire left Ben to tidy up.

When Claire saw the large steel slide, she became lost in her own world. Rosie removed her sunglasses and sat down at a shady picnic table with Will.

'How's everything been since last week?' she asked.

'Good. I'm still off work, so I'm just resting up.'

'Resting up? You look exhausted. Have you actually been sleeping?'

'Yeah, it's fine,' Will lied. The last week was a blur, but he was feeling the strain of his recovery, and all he'd seen with the fire. He just had to relax while he was here, and forget all the craziness. He'd already scared Rosie once. He would not do it again.

'The police caught those kids,' he said.

Rosie perked up. 'Oh, that's great. They deserve to have the book thrown at them for what they did! You could've died.'

'They're just kids. It doesn't matter, anyway – it's over now.'

'Every day, the news reports on some horrible crime happening in Sydney. I don't like you living there by yourself,' Rosie said, as she put her arm around Will.

'I know you don't.'

It was all he could say. There was no point trying to defend the city – the crime rates spoke for themselves, and now Will was part of those statistics.

After a moment of silence, Rosie changed the subject.

'So… are you dating anyone?' she asked, with a smirk.

'Like last time, the answer's no.' He gently nudged her shoulder.

'Oh, come on. Get out there and find someone!'

'The more you push, the longer it'll take me.'

They laughed, before sitting back and watching Claire play.

When she'd run around for another half an hour, and scared Rosie half to death by repeatedly trying to hang upside down from the monkey bars, she'd finally exhausted herself. Will spent the rest of the day catching up with Ben and being shown every new toy Claire had received since Christmas.

After dinner, she begged Will to read her a bedtime story. He was happy to oblige, and sat on the edge of her bed as she produced a frayed retelling of Jack and the Beanstalk.

'I remember this book,' Will said. 'My mum – I mean, Grandma – used to read this to me and Rosie when we were little.'

'Mum has lots of them,' Claire replied eagerly.

Will was glad Rosie had kept their mother's books, and was reading them to her daughter. Still, seeing one made him a little sad. He missed his mother every day. After she'd died, he'd felt incredibly alone, especially with Rosie so far away. It had always just been the three of them. Will's mother had never remarried, and had always refused to speak about his father. As a child, he'd been curious, but as he'd grown older it'd been replaced by anger at the man who'd abandoned them. All Will had ever seen of his father was an old photo taken on their wedding day. He found it hard to miss someone he'd never known, who'd never wanted to know him.

Claire fell asleep halfway through the story. Softly, Will placed the book on the bedside table, switched off the light, and crept out of the room. He returned to the kitchen and gave Rosie and Ben a thumbs-up.

'Fast asleep,' he said.

'Thanks.' Rosie kicked her shoes off to the side of the kitchen. 'We're almost done cleaning up here, and are thinking of watching a movie. Any preferences?'

'Nah, I don't mind. I just want to get changed – I've been in these clothes all day. Back in a minute.'

'I'll make you a cup of tea,' Rosie called, as he left to the guest bedroom.

Sitting on the edge of the bed, Will took his shoes off. On a shelf just above eye level was a familiar statue of a woman. It had been his mother's. She'd kept it in a glass cabinet in the living room of his family home, after falling in love with it in an antique shop. It was about seven inches tall and made of porcelain, with long black hair, a pale blue dress, and a yellow flower in its hand. It must've been at least a hundred years old, but was beautifully crafted.

When Will stood, he felt suddenly dizzy. The room was moving as if he'd just spun on the spot. As he sat back on the bed to gather himself, he noticed his mother's statue move. It was the only thing in focus, and seemed to have doubled in size, now just barely fitting on the shelf.

Rope came out from behind the statue, and wrapped around its smooth body. As the rope wound tighter and tighter, Will heard a muffled sound. It was distant, but there was no mistaking it – a woman was trying to speak through something, as if her mouth was gagged.

Will stared at the statue, waiting for more information. He allowed himself to be totally immersed in what he was seeing, desperate to solve the riddle wrapping around his mother's keepsake.

It wobbled on the shelf, trying to free itself from the restraints that were becoming tighter and tighter. The stifled voice continued. Will couldn't figure out what it was saying, but it sounded distressed. Stretching out as far as he could, he tried to touch it, while still glued to the edge of the bed. Just as he felt he might get there, the statue shrunk back to its regular size and the room returned to normal. Will's legs were functioning again, and he quickly stood and picked up his mother's statue. It was unbound, cold and lifeless.

Will breathed deeply as he tried to commit everything he'd seen to memory. He didn't want a repeat of the fire – but again, he was taunted with titbits of nonsensical information.

Rosie and Ben were waiting for him, scrolling through Netflix on the TV. Leaving the bedroom, he shuffled down the hall toward them. He still felt a little dazed, and didn't want Rosie to think anything was wrong, or she'd start worrying again.

Halfway to the living room, Will heard the woman's voice again. Though it was louder this time, he still couldn't make out what she was trying to say. He stopped dead in his tracks. Hanging on the wall was a watercolour of Sydney Harbour, which Rosie had bought herself to remind her of the city. It was beautifully done, and detailed both the Sydney Opera House and the Harbour Bridge as seen from Kirribilli. Will was drawn to the painting, as if in a trance. Moving toward it, he realised what the voice was saying.

Help. Over and over again. Help. It echoed through his mind.

He leaned in until he was inches away from the painting, desperate to learn more. He wouldn't forgive himself if he let this go the same way as the fire.

The watercolours began to swirl and blend, losing all of their brightness. After a moment, he was looking at a cold, concrete industrial scene of a warehouse with the number eleven written over its large metal doors. In the background, he could see water, and a plane taking off.

He knew exactly what he was looking at. The shipping area of Port Botany, just behind Sydney Airport. Before working at the hospital, Will had done some general labouring around the docks, packing boxes into delivery trucks. There was no mistaking it.

Will reached out and touched the painting. The canvas was dry. As he ran his fingers over the warehouse, the muffled pleas in his head grew louder.

Someone was inside that warehouse, crying for help.

Pulling back, Will saw the landscape watercolour of Sydney Harbour, exactly as it should be. His heart was racing. Finally, the random images made sense.

He remembered Detective Woods. He wouldn't call the emergency line – they'd think he was crazy – but Detective Woods had heard him describe Tony Hartley without ever having seen him. Will knew what he'd seen, and he trusted himself. He just had to convince Woods to do the same.

THIRTEEN

It had been almost a full day since Abby was taken, and the adrenaline which had been pumping through Martin Sullivan's veins was running out. He hadn't slept since her kidnapping, and felt nauseous with exhaustion and guilt. He feared the worst. Even if he made the payment for Abby's release, would he ever see her again?

Martin stared at the blank flat-screen TV mounted on his living room wall. As he sat quietly, hugging a cushion with his phone in hand, a team of detectives busied themselves throughout the house. It now resembled some kind of command post, with computers, phones, and wires taking every available space. The police had spent the entire day coming and going, and most of them busied themselves with their fancy equipment, paying him no attention at all. Earlier, a group of crime scene officers had gone through every inch of the house with tiny brushes, leaving it covered in black fingerprint powder. They'd worked for hours, but despite all their efforts, Martin had overheard an officer say there was nothing to be found.

Just after midday, Detectives Woods, Lapis, Yule and O'Donnell had returned. They planned to stay with Martin during the night, still expecting a call from the kidnappers. However, the longer Martin sat there without hearing his phone ring, the more he doubted his wife was still alive.

Now, Yule introduced Martin to Sergeant Oxford, a well-dressed, lanky police negotiator with thinning hair. Yule had brough him in to coach Martin on what to say when the call came through. For Abby's sake, Martin gave Oxford his full attention.

'We want them to talk, so we can learn as much as possible,' Sergeant Oxford said, as he removed his suit jacket and sat on the couch next to Martin. 'Don't concern yourself with the actual phone trace. Remember, the more they talk, the greater the chance they'll give something up about themselves. If you get stuck, just tell them about Abby. Try to personalise her.'

'Okay, anything else?' Martin asked, trying his best to take all the advice on board.

'It's very important we hear from Abby. We need to make sure she's okay. Also, we really need the payment information – just in case.'

'I'll pay whatever they want to get her back.'

'I know,' Oxford said. 'Look, that's all I'll say for now. We need you to be dynamic – too much planning can cause problems if they go off script.'

Martin's phone rang.

The room froze, and all conversations came to an immediate halt. Martin looked to the detectives for guidance. There was a second of quiet chaos as everyone rushed to their places. Detective Woods sat on Martin's other side, and Detective Yule nodded for him to answer the call.

'This is Martin Sullivan,' he said, as his whole body trembled uncontrollably.

'Listen carefully, Mr Sullivan,' said a deep, artificial-sounding voice.

Detective Sergeant O'Donnell, who was listening to the call through a pair of headphones, mouthed *voice box* to Yule. Yule nodded.

'I have no intention of saying much, so here's your wife to do some talking. Proof that she is still alive. I'm a man of my word, Mr Sullivan. If you do as I tell you, I will not hurt her.'

Martin heard Abby's muffled voice, and burst into tears.

'Please, let her go. I'll send you the money.'

'Very good,' the deep voice continued. 'Now, I hope you have a pen ready for the wallet ID.'

'What can I call you?' Martin asked. Sergeant Oxford gave him a thumbs-up.

'Listen carefully, because I am only going to give you the wallet address once. I suggest you pay attention instead of asking questions. If you don't write it down correctly, I won't receive my money, and your wife will be dead.'

Martin choked a little, but held back more tears. He gestured for a pen, and Detective Woods handed him one, along with a notepad.

'I'm ready.'

Slowly, the voice dictated the 28-character, alphanumeric Bitcoin wallet address.

'Got it?'

'Yes,' Martin replied.

'In exactly twenty-four hours, you will transfer a minimum of 28.572 Bitcoin to that wallet. Once I have received it, I will contact you again, and arrange for Abby to be returned. It is really quite simple. I hope neither you nor the police listening in do anything that will cause Abby to be harmed.'

The call ended.

Martin began hyperventilating. Woods tried to calm him down, while the rest of the team rushed over to O'Donnell, who sat by a laptop and interpreted the call data.

'Shit!' O'Donnell yelled, as he tore off his headphones. 'The call must've come from a VoIP application using data, because it didn't use the phone lines.'

'So we don't know where it came from?'

'No. Dammit. What was the number?' O'Donnell asked Martin.

Martin was sitting bolt upright, still silently panicking. He handed the phone to O'Donnell.

'It's from a +86 number, hang on a sec.' O'Donnell got back on the computer. 'Japan. Shit!'

'Alright,' Yule said, 'I want someone to call the Australian Embassy over in Japan now. We'll get the local cops to look into that number.'

Yule flopped into the armchair beside the couch and rubbed his forehead.

'They can't trace it, can they?' Martin asked Woods.

'We're going to keep working on that, okay? Don't give up hope. What's important is that Abby's still alive,' she said.

Martin buried his head in his hands. For the first time, he requested to be alone.

The team made their way out. Detective Woods was the last to leave, and told Martin to call if he needed anything. Striding down the hall, she saw the detectives sitting around the kitchen table in silence. She kept going, pushing out the door and into the backyard. The night was cold, but the fresh air was welcoming after being stuck all day in a room with far too many people. As she drew in a deep breath, her phone rang. She didn't recognise the number.

'Detective Aubrey Woods.'

'It's Will Denham,' Will said, voice frantic. 'I really need to talk to you.'

'This isn't a good time.'

'Please, just wait. Hear me out.'

'What happened to you at the hospital?'

'Oh, it was just a misunderstanding – after the attack, I wasn't really myself. I'm out now, but that's not why I'm calling.'

Woods looked back toward the house and saw the detectives still sitting silently around the kitchen table.

'Okay, what's up?' she asked.

'It's hard to say, but just hear me out. You know all that stuff I said about Tony Hartley—'

'Will, seriously! I don't have time for this. I'm working a case tonight.'

'I saw something else, just now. A warehouse in Botany. I saw ropes and heard a woman screaming, but it was muffled. I think someone's in trouble.'

Woods snapped to attention. 'What?'

'Warehouse number eleven at the international shipping port. That's what I saw.'

'What do you mean, you saw it? What happened?'

'I saw a flash of the warehouse, and a muffled scream was coming from inside.'

'You aren't making any sense. What's going on?'

'I don't know, I wish I did. But you need to trust me.'

Woods was getting impatient. 'Trust you? I barely know you, and you're sounding ridiculous.'

'Please, Aubrey,' Will said. 'Just check it out. Something isn't right there.'

Woods frantically searched for logic in what Will was saying. Could he be talking about the kidnapping?

'What do you know about this warehouse?'

'Nothing, but I know what I saw. Just like with the fire.'

Woods sighed and lowered her voice. She didn't want her colleagues to hear this conversation.

'Do you know how crazy you sound right now?'

'Yes, but please, check it out. Warehouse eleven. Someone could be in real trouble.'

Woods paused to think. During the silence, she could hear Will panting in through the phone, as though something had got him worked up. He sounded insane, but she couldn't help thinking – what if, by some chance, it was related to Abby Sullivan?

Woods's mind raced. Had Will actually seen something, but was too afraid to say, so instead made up this absurd story to get her to look into it? Or maybe he was involved?

She chose her next words very carefully.

'Do you know what case I'm on right now?'

'I didn't even know you were working. I just needed to tell someone what I saw, and didn't know who else to call.'

'Does the name Abby Sullivan mean anything to you?'

'No. Should it?'

Woods ignored the question and thought some more.

'Okay. Fine. I'll check out this warehouse.'

Will exhaled. 'Thank you. Please tell me if you find anything.'

Woods ended the call and bit her lip, frustrated with herself for agreeing to look into something that made no sense at all. Clearly, Will was having some issues, but the investigator in her refused to ignore the chance that he had information about someone in trouble, whether it was Abby Sullivan or not. Either she could sit in this house all night and wonder what to do next, or take a quick drive and be back before anyone realised she was gone.

Woods strode back into the house and past the kitchen. She called for Lapis to follow her into the hall.

'Hey, I'm just going to go check something out. I won't be long.'

'You all good? Want me to come with you?'

'No, it's fine. It's just for that drug case I've been working on,' she said. 'I want to do a quick drive-by of a suspect's house while it's all quiet here. I'll be back within the hour.'

'Okay. Call me if you need anything.'

As Woods got in her car, she shook her head, still surprised she'd agreed to go along with this. She'd considered telling Lapis about the call with Will, but she didn't need her colleagues thinking she too was losing her mind.

It was only a short drive from Paddington to Port Botany, and Woods found the entrance to the docks easily enough. Although it was almost 9 p.m., there was still plenty of work being done, with huge cranes swinging cargo containers and several trucks backing up. She wove through the maze of shipping containers until she saw a long row of rusted warehouses. Slowly, she drove down the line. The numbers were sequential, starting with warehouse number fifty-five. Eleven was toward the end, near the water. She stopped the car and got out.

From the outside, number eleven looked like every other warehouse she'd driven past, aside for the fact that its main door was ajar. She pointed her torch toward it. There was a gap about two inches wide, where the door wasn't latched all the way across. Woods put her ear to the small opening.

A light scratching sound echoed from within the warehouse. Her heart raced as she recalled her building entry training, visualising the best way to get inside and maintain a tactical advantage. Suddenly, she wished she hadn't come alone.

Woods drew her gun. Trying to keep her trembling hands steady, she opened the door a little more with the tip of her torch, so she could see all the way inside. The scratching noise continued. Before she could second-guess herself, she flung the doors open and entered, announcing her office as loudly as she could, pointing her gun into the centre of the room.

The warehouse was completely empty. Just a concrete floor, steel walls, and fluorescent lights hanging from the rafters above. As Woods explored the vast space with her torch, she saw two well-fed brown rats scurrying away from the beam of light, scratching the floor as they ran. Feeling foolish, and trying to settle her adrenaline, she switched the torch off and returned to her car.

Just as she reached it, she saw a dock worker on a forklift heading in her direction. She held out her badge and switched her torch back on, the light reflecting off his bright fluorescent vest. He stopped and took off his hard hat.

'Hi, officer. Everything okay?'

'Just making some enquiries. Warehouse eleven over there, you know who uses it?'

'Nope, sorry.'

'Have you seen anyone enter or leave it recently?'

'No, I don't think that place has been used for a while.'

'Yeah, didn't think so. Thanks.'

As Woods drove away from the abandoned warehouse, she cursed Will for wasting her time, and cursed herself for listening to him.

***

Forty minutes ago, in that same warehouse, Evans ended the call with Martin Sullivan.

'Let's go,' he said.

Pollard removed the ropes holding Abby to an old chair, threw her over his shoulder, and lay her on the backseat of their new car – a grey seven-seated Land Cruiser, recently acquired by Pollard. With a pillowcase over her head and tape across her mouth, Abby had no idea what was happening. She kicked and squealed with every ounce of energy she had left, but was no match against Pollard, who retied the thick rope around her ankles and wrists before shutting the back door.

After checking the empty warehouse one last time, Evans packed more rope and the wooden chair into the boot of the car.

'What did you make of the call?' Pollard asked.

'It went well. Sullivan will pay on time.'

'What about the police? They'll work out that we called from here.' Pollard scanned the warehouse, making sure they'd left absolutely no trace of their presence.

'I told you not to worry about that. Even if they could trace the call, by the time they got here, we'd be long gone.'

'Moving around just seems risky,' Pollard said.

'So is staying in one spot. I've got it all worked out, and I don't need to explain myself to you. I'm not paying you for your opinion.'

'Fine. Let's get going, then.'

Their next destination was a three-hour drive away. Evans hadn't even told Pollard where they were going, but trusted all the arrangements would be made.

Things were going exactly as planned.

FOURTEEN

After Will got off the phone with Woods, he crept back into the hall and stared at the watercolour of Sydney Harbour. He desperately wanted to see the warehouse again, or have some other glimpse of information.

Although he watched the painting for five minutes, it remained the original vivid and wonderful landscape. He tried everything to get his mind working again. He tapped the painting, stroked it, put his nose right against the canvas, even pleaded with it to show him more. Nothing.

Back in the guest room, Will picked up his mother's statue. As a child, he'd been forbidden from touching his mother's china, so holding the fragile statue felt unnatural. Still, he could appreciate how beautiful it was. The craftsmanship was superb, the lines of the woman's face and body made with precision.

No matter how hard he wished for something more, he saw only the statue. He saw no ropes and heard no voices. Gently, he put her back on the shelf, and sat on the bed.

He was too worked up to sleep, but too distracted to sit with Rosie and Ben. The call to Woods had left him buzzing with anticipation. Whatever was happening inside the warehouse, he hoped she was being careful.

As the time neared 1 a.m., Will started wondering what was taking her so long. He tried calling her again, but it went straight to voicemail. He hung up without leaving a message, not wanting to interrupt whatever she was dealing with, and eventually fell asleep.

Early the next morning, Will woke. He'd forgotten to shut the bedroom blinds all the way, and as the sun rose, it flooded the room with light. Before any other thought came to him, he reached over to check his phone. No missed calls, no messages.

Will sat up. It was only 6 a.m., but he called Detective Woods again. He needed to know what she'd found. Again, it went straight to voicemail, and he left a message for her to call with an update.

His mother's statue was still on the shelf. Had it moved at all, or had his mind just made it happen? He picked it up and examined it, trying to make something happen, but it remained still. As he passed the painting of Sydney Harbour, he gave it another deep stare. Nothing.

Ben was sitting by the kitchen table helping Claire with her breakfast, while Rosie was making coffee. All three were dressed and ready for their day, in contrast to Will, who wore an old singlet and baggy tracksuit pants.

'Morning. Why are you all up so early?' he asked, rubbing his eyes.

'Good morning,' Ben said. Claire tried to say something similar through a mouth full of porridge.

Rosie pulled another mug out for Will, and poured him some coffee. 'It's a beautiful day – why waste it? How'd you sleep? I hope that room wasn't too dusty, it doesn't get used much.'

'No, it was fine.' As Will took the mug, Claire looked at him and patted the chair next to her. He sat down and helped himself to some toast.

'Thanks for having me, guys,' he said. 'I really appreciate it, but I think I'm going to head back home this morning.'

'No!' Claire shouted.

'Claire, don't yell,' Rosie scolded, before turning to her brother. 'Really, Will? I was hoping you'd stay the entire weekend.' She wasn't hiding her disappointment.

'Yeah, stay,' Ben said. 'It's going to be a really nice day.'

'I forgot about some things I need to sort out back home. Getting ready to go back to work, stuff like that. But I had a great time, and I promise I won't leave it this long to visit again.'

'At least have some breakfast before you head back,' Rosie said.

'Yeah, of course.'

After they ate, Will excused himself to pack his things. In the bedroom, he checked his phone again, but there was still no response from Detective Woods. What if he'd sent her into something dangerous? If someone had injured a police officer, it would've been a big story, but he found nothing when he scrolled through his social media and several news websites. Finally, he decided he was overthinking it. After all, it was still early. He'd probably receive a call back from Woods later in the day.

He finished throwing everything into his backpack and headed to the kitchen to say his goodbyes. Claire gave him a big hug and asked him to just move in, so he'd always be home. Ben walked him and Rosie to the car.

The first minute of the ride was quiet.

'Why are you really leaving early?' Rosie asked, as she turned down the radio.

'Like I said, I forgot I have some things to do at home,' Will replied, staring out the window.

'I don't buy it. Something's not right – you haven't been yourself since you got here.'

'Honestly, I'm okay.'

Will wanted to tell her everything. She'd always been the person he could count on most, but he knew, just like Ravi, she'd take some convincing. He didn't have the energy to even try, let alone find proof to back up what she'd think was madness or a lame joke.

They rode the rest of the way in silence. When they got to the station, he kissed her on the cheek and thanked her again.

Waiting for the next train, Will checked his phone. There was still nothing from Detective Woods. Instead of continuing to try to contact her, he decided to call Ravi.

Ravi picked up on the first few rings. Will told him to prepare for some strange news, before recounting everything he'd seen and heard the night before.

'That's incredible,' Ravi said. 'What do you think it meant?'

'I have no idea, but I told the detective who handled my assault case.'

'You told someone else? They believed it?'

'I told her some things about the fire I shouldn't have been able to know, but she doesn't buy it all. Still, she agreed to check it out – I think she didn't want to risk missing something. Plus, she said she's on some major case at the moment. Maybe it's connected.'

'What's the case?'

'No idea. She didn't say.'

'Have you heard anything since she went there? What did she find?'

'I tried calling her last night and this morning, but she hasn't got back to me yet.' Will paced up and down the empty platform. 'I have to talk to her. I'm not going to let someone get hurt like last time.'

'Can I do anything to help?'

'Not at the moment,' Will said. 'I'm going to get in touch with her and find out what's going on.'

'Call me when you do. Oh, and Will?'

'Yeah?'

'I'm still trying to work out why this is happening to you.

There's some research about neurological anticipation in humans – really basic precognition, like gut feelings. You're on a whole new level, though. If you get any new symptoms, or something changes, please tell me right away. Whatever's going on, I need to make sure it isn't hurting you.'

FIFTEEN

As the train rolled away from Queanbeyan Station, Will stared out the window and thought about what Ravi had said. He'd never considered any side effects of what was happening to him – he'd been too preoccupied with working out the meaning of the visions. Strange and exhausting as they were, he wanted them to happen more often.

As the train picked up speed, Will decided the best thing to do was to keep his mind open. To touch things and speak to people, to stimulate and expand his consciousness.

He arrived back at Central Station just before midday. On the short walk home, he was reminded how different the city was from the rural area he'd just left. It was noisy, the streets busy with cars and pedestrians, and though it was a sunny day, he walked in the constant chill shadow of the tall buildings overhead. Still, he was enjoying being home.

Back at his building, Will bumped into Mrs Simmons, who was tending the communal garden near the entrance. He touched the petals of different-coloured flowers while she commented on how well he looked and how quickly he was recovering. When it became clear that nothing was going to happen there, he wished Mrs Simmons a nice day and climbed the stairs to his apartment.

He threw his bag down and went straight for the bathroom. The site of the first vision might hold some value. He turned on the taps, stood in the bath, and stared deep into the mirror, but saw only himself. Running into the living room, he touched everything he could see. Again, nothing happened.

Frustrated, he flopped onto the couch and switched on the TV. As he tried to decide what to watch, his pocket vibrated. He pulled out his ringing phone. The caller ID was a number he recognised – Detective Woods.

'What happened at the warehouse?' he asked, before she could speak.

'It was completely empty,' she replied coldly. 'That's what happened. I can't believe I wasted my time on your stupid tip.'

'What do you mean, empty? That's impossible. I know what I saw.'

'You know what you saw?' she replied, in a mocking tone. 'You're insane, and I'm just as bad for believing it.'

'But are you sure? Did you go to the right place?'

'Yes, I'm not an idiot. Next time you think you see something, don't call me. Call a doctor.'

'Detective, I'm sorry, I—'

'Spare me, Will. I'm not interested.'

Woods hung up. Just as he was about to call her back, he stopped himself. He knew she wouldn't answer.

It made no sense. Will felt sick, knowing someone was still out there, needing help.

He called Ravi.

'Hey, did you hear from the detective?'

'Yeah, and she wasn't happy,' Will said. 'She told me the warehouse was empty, but I feel like something's missing. I'm going to go and check it out.'

'Well, I'm coming. You might need help – you never know what you'll run into.'

'Bring a first aid kit from the hospital. From what I saw,

someone could be in real trouble.'

Will had idea what he was going to do at the warehouse, or what he would find, but he needed to see it for himself. Although the sun was still out, it offered no warmth. He pulled on his thickest jacket and went to meet Ravi.

It was the weekend, so Port Botany wasn't as busy as usual, but there were still workers around. All of them looked pretty calm and casual. Will suspected they were either waiting for a shipment to arrive, or their boss was off for the day, so they were taking it easy.

'Where to?' Ravi asked, as the car crawled through a seemingly endless maze of cargo containers.

'Head to the left and go all the way to the end. That's where the warehouses are,' Will replied, remembering the long days and nights he'd spent working there.

Ravi drove on slowly. After a few hundred metres, they reached a stretch of old steel warehouses. The closer they got to the water, the more the warehouses suffered from severe rust and salt damage. Will kept a lookout for their numbers.

'Here! Stop the car, this is it.'

They'd arrived in front of warehouse eleven, which perfectly resembled what he'd seen in Rosie's painting. He jumped out of the car when Ravi was still coming to a stop.

'Just the way I saw it,' he said.

The only way in or out seemed to be by the large sliding doors at the front. When they reached the entrance, Will and Ravi nodded at each other. Will grabbed one handle and slid it to the side. He only needed to open the door a few feet to see that the warehouse was completely empty.

'There's nothing here,' he said. Woods had been right. She'd wasted her time – no wonder she'd been angry.

'I'm sorry, mate,' Ravi said, looking just as disappointed as

Will felt.

'Why did I see this warehouse? Why did I see ropes, and hear screaming? What does it all mean? Maybe it's a sign, but I can't work it out,' Will said, getting more frustrated by the minute.

'Let's go inside and look around. It might help.'

Will entered the warehouse first. There were no windows, and the only light came through the open door. He found a switch, and several fluorescent lights hanging from the rafters flickered on, giving a dim, humming glow. Although he'd found the outside of the warehouse instantly recognisable, the inside felt completely foreign.

'Anything?' Ravi asked. His voice echoed through the space.

'No.' Will stared through the cold, empty building, before letting out a deep sigh. 'Come on, let's get out of here.'

He paced along the row of warehouses. There was no mistaking what he'd seen, but he wasn't sure if it had already happened, or was about to. Fifty metres away was the long concrete pier where ships docked to unload their cargo. The sea was calm, and the powerful sunlight reflected off the surface, creating a bright glare.

As Will approached, the surface became choppy. The sky grew darker, and the wind picked up. Waves thrashed against the concrete dock until it was swallowed by whitewash, and a spray of cold water flicked his face.

He turned back to Ravi, who was leaning on his car.

'Let's go. Storm's on the way,' Will called, raising his voice over the crashing waves.

'Huh?' Ravi replied.

'The waves,' he said, pointing back toward the sea.

'What're you talking about?' There's barely a breeze out there.'

Will hurried away from the water. Ravi kept a close eye on

him, and appeared to work out what was happening at the same time he did. Turning back, Will saw that the ocean had returned to its previous level of calm. He glanced at Ravi, but neither said anything.

As he looked beyond the car, down what seemed to be an endless stretch of identical steel warehouses, Will felt suddenly detached from all of it. The world turned dark and windy. He walked past Ravi, eyes focusing on the long stretch of road ahead.

Two people appeared in front of him. Will didn't recognise either of them, but one was large, muscular, and covered in tattoos, while the other was shorter and more slender, with a clean-cut, professional look. They were running, getting further away from Will by the second. It was hard to see them through the darkness, and he felt a strong desire to catch up.

A muffled cry split the gloom. Will knew what was happening, and refused to miss the chance to find out where it was coming from. He sprinted to reach the pair. The harder he pushed himself, the louder the screams became. His sides were aching, and he was barely able to see through the darkness, but he kept going. As he ran, the concrete under his feet turned into lush grass, and the warehouses disappeared, replaced with open fields illuminated only by a bright full moon.

Wind whipped his face. He sprinted onwards, long grass flicking against his ankles, heading toward the two men and the stifled screams. He did his best to keep up, but the men were too fast. Before long, he lost sight of them in a distant black haze.

As Will stood with his hands on his head, drawing in deep breaths, the muffled voice sounded again. This time, it was directly behind him, and more piercing than it had ever been. He spun around to find thick, dark fog instead of the empty field he'd just run through. As he strode into it, following the screams, it cleared. Daylight replaced the glow of the moon, illuminating the same farmland he'd just seen in the blackness of night. Jogging through the thick grass, he saw a small caravan, rusty and dilapidated, underneath several dense trees. He ran toward its door, but couldn't find a handle. The muffled screaming continued from inside, along with the sound of bare skin being slapped and male voices yelling. Will banged on the walls as hard as he could, shouting, but no one came out.

He circled the caravan, looking for a way inside, or a crack to peer through, but there were none. Every window had been boarded up with wooden planks. A long dirt road led away from the caravan. Its sides were lined in fog, and he could only see straight down it.

Deciding there was no way in, Will sprinted along the dusty path. After a long run, he reached its end, which intersected with a sealed bitumen road. He was entirely surrounded by thick fog. The caravan was out of sight. As he tried to catch his breath, he glanced up and saw a street sign pointing down the dirt path. Underneath the street name, Berry Drive, was some smaller text: Stubbo – Mid-Western Regional Council.

Will gasped and fell to the ground. Groggily, he looked around and saw he was back in the corridor of warehouses.

'Will, you okay?' Ravi asked, checking his pulse and looking into his eyes. 'Talk to me. What happened?'

'Whoa... I'm back,' Will said. Rubbing his face, he staggered to a stand, with Ravi supporting his arms.

'You're back? What do you mean?'

'I'm calling Detective Woods,' Will said. 'I need to convince her I'm right this time. I don't know why I saw the warehouse first, but I know where the woman is.'

SIXTEEN

Detective Sergeant Ian Yule strode into the conference room on the first floor of Surry Hills Police Station. Following behind was Detective Chief Inspector Blake Munro, coordinator of the Robbery and Serious Crime Squad, who was overseeing the investigation. Munro was a red-haired, forty-year veteran of the police force. He'd seen just about every crime there was, but in this case, like Yule, he was unsettled by the precision of the two kidnappers.

'Listen up, everyone,' Yule said. The room was filled with detectives from the station and the Robbery Squad, but it silenced the moment that he spoke, and stragglers hurried to find their chairs. 'Just to recap, Abby Sullivan has now been missing for almost two days, and the deadline for payment is creeping up on us fast. Aside from the one phone call Martin Sullivan received from the kidnappers, we've had no communication with them. We have no leads and no forensic evidence.'

The crowd rumbled, as detectives began to argue over what the next step should be.

'Quiet, please,' Yule said. The chatter ceased immediately. 'Now, we know the caller's number originated from Japan. We reached out to our colleagues over there, and they ran it for us. It's registered to a "Happytime Industries" in Takayama, which doesn't exist, and is probably an attempt at mockery.' Pulling some paperwork from a folder, Yule continued. 'The guys over at Cybercrime have told me the sim card was likely purchased on the dark web. Chances are, they used data roaming with a VPN to make the call, while changing their geographic location. They could've set their location anywhere in the world.'

Yule put the paperwork down on the table in front of him and turned to Munro.

'You all know Detective Chief Inspector Munro. I'll pass things over to him.'

'Thanks. Team, we don't have time on our side.' Munro's voice was deep, and just as commanding as Yule's. 'Until we hear otherwise, we treat the kidnappers' threat as serious, and assume that Mrs Sullivan will be killed unless they receive payment. I've spoken to Mr Sullivan, and he's prepared to make the payment tonight if there are no other options.'

Again, the crowd began to murmur.

'I know it isn't ideal, but our priority is to make sure Mrs Sullivan isn't hurt. In the meantime, I want all of you to keep investigating the list of associates Mr Sullivan has given us.'

The detectives wrote the instructions down in their notepads. There were over sixty names that needed to be checked.

'We will not give up on this case,' Munro said. 'Even if the ransom is paid, and Abby is returned, we will keep working until we find the people responsible.' He clapped sharply. 'Now, get to work.'

✳ ✳ ✳

As Evans drove down Berry Drive, he felt he'd ticked every box and done everything according to plan. An associate of his had been discreetly cooking meth in the dingy old caravan for years. No one knew it was there, and their arrival in Stubbo had been covered by cold and windy weather, which had kept the locals tucked away in their homes. They'd be safe hiding out in the caravan. Once the ransom payment was received, they'd ditch Abby a few kilometres from Stubbo and drive further west.

That plan changed as soon as he parked the stolen Land Cruiser.

On the long drive from Botany to Stubbo, Evans and Pollard had removed their balaclavas and covered Abby with a thick blue tarpaulin. To anyone passing by, it would've looked like two mates heading into the country for a camping trip. Abby had been quiet in the backseat, seemingly sleeping or unconscious.

When they arrived, Pollard opened the back door and was met with her face-to-face. Somehow, she'd untied herself under the tarp and removed her hood and mouth gag. She looked directly into Pollard's eyes, then over to Evans. Seeing an opportunity, she didn't hesitate, kicking Pollard in the genitals as hard as she could and running past his withering body. Evans sprinted after her.

Collecting himself, Pollard retrieved a small pistol from the back of his pants, turned the safety off, and joined the chase. Abby was fast, but she hadn't eaten or drunk in days. As she raced across the barren farmland, screaming as loudly as she could, the two men caught up and tackled her into the ground. Abby fought hard, but she was no match for them.

While she was still on the ground, Pollard pushed his pistol against her temple.

'No!' Evans yelled. He shoved Pollard's arm. Pollard stared furiously back at him, but put the gun away.

With a quick punch to the back of Abby's head, Pollard knocked her unconscious. Evans stood over her incapacitated body, returning Pollard's deep and hostile stare.

'How did she get herself loose?' he spat, still catching his breath.

'I don't know,' Pollard said. 'I thought I made the ropes tight.'

'Obviously not tight enough, you stupid prick! Look what's happened. She almost got away – and now she's seen our faces!'

'We have to kill her,' Pollard said coldly.

'Jesus!' Evans ran his fingers through his slicked-back hair. His plan had been going perfectly, and now it was unravelling right in front of him. He wasn't a murderer. This was not supposed to happen. 'And you brought a gun?'

'I always carry it. Lucky for us, too.'

Evans crouched next to Abby and rubbed his forehead.

'She was never meant to die, and here you are, pushing a gun in her face.'

'Well, what choice do we have? She's seen us,' Pollard said. 'She can ID us now. I'm not going back to prison.'

'Just let me think.'

'No!' Pollard shouted, grabbing Evans by the scruff of his shirt and lifting him back to his feet. 'Shit happens. Things don't go as you expect, and now I'm taking over to clean this mess up and save the both of us. Once the money comes in, we shoot her and dump the body where they'll never find it.'

Evans pulled himself away from Pollard's grip.

His partner was right. He was reluctant to admit it, but there was no other option.

'Fine,' he said. 'We kill her.'

SEVENTEEN

After being dismissed from Yule's briefing, Woods collected her notes and made her way out of the conference room.

'You think Sullivan will end up paying?' Lapis asked.

'It's not looking real good, and this pile of names is going to take a long time to cross-check. I think he'll have to.'

'Makes me feel pretty useless, really.'

'Look, you heard the boss,' Woods said. 'Even after the payment's made, we'll keep working on it. The Robbery Squad will probably take the case back to headquarters, but I'm going to see if I can stay on it with them.'

'Good luck with that. We're short-staffed as it is – I'm not sure they'd let you leave, even if it's only temporary.'

'You know I want to get out of here and work on bigger cases. It could be a good opportunity for me.'

'You're a good detective, Aubrey. You'll get your chance.'

Woods and Lapis walked back to their office and dropped their notepads on their desks.

'We're going to be here a while, by the look of things,' Woods said. 'You want to come and grab something to eat before we start?'

'Nah, you go. I want to at least try to make it home for dinner tonight. My wife will kill me if I bail again.'

'Well, I've got nowhere to go, so I'll bunker down as long as they need me. I don't want to leave until I know Abby's safe.'

At her favourite small cafe, just around the corner on Oxford Street, Woods sat by the window while she waited for her food. As she gazed toward the street, watching traffic, she heard her phone ring.

'Detective Aubrey Woods,' she answered.

'Hi. It's Will Denham again.'

Woods let out a loud, exhausted sigh. She was passionate about her work, but moments like this made her reconsider handing her business card out too liberally. Will had seemed normal when they first met, but the more she got to know him, the more she wanted to block his number.

'What do you want?'

'Look, I know you're angry about the warehouse, but you have to trust me on this one. There's a woman being held hostage. I saw it all, clear as anything, exactly like last time. There were two men with her. One had a gun. I think she's in real trouble, and—'

'You have to stop this!' Woods snapped. A few cafe patrons glanced over at her, so she stood and stalked outside. 'And exactly like last time? Where'd that get me? An empty warehouse, that's where.'

'I'm not making this up. I saw the two men – I ran after them, and found an old caravan. The woman was in there. Please, if not for me, do it for her. She needs help.'

'There is no woman, Will. I promise you, if you keep ringing me with this rubbish, I'm going to arrest you for harassment.'

***

'Dammit!' Will hissed, as he lowered his phone. 'She hung up on me. I mean, I can't blame her, but this is someone's life at stake.'

He and Ravi paced around the dock near warehouse eleven,

trying to work out what to do next.

'I think I have an idea,' Ravi said. 'But I need you to be sure of what you saw. Totally sure.'

'Of course, I told you everything right after it happened. It's still fresh in my mind.'

'The two men, the caravan, the gun, the street sign. Everything's correct, yeah?'

'Yes, absolutely. What're you getting at?'

'Get in the car. I'll explain on the way.'

As Ravi drove back through the front gates, Will pressed him for answers.

'So, what's this plan of yours?'

'I need to find a payphone first. There has to be one around here somewhere.'

'No one uses payphones anymore.'

'You're going to use one. Ah, there.' Ravi stopped the car by some shops on the main road. Before them was an old payphone, covered in graffiti. 'Perfect.'

'Okay, fill me in. What are you thinking?'

'You call 000 and tell them what you saw.'

'I can't do that! They'll think I'm crazy.'

'No, don't tell them you saw it in your head. Say you actually watched it happen. You're a local farmer who drove past and saw it.'

'If I get caught...'

Ravi cut him off. 'You're totally sure of what you saw, right? You trust yourself completely?'

'Of course I do,' Will replied.

'Then there's no issue. Use a fake name – it's a payphone, so they won't know it's you – and then they'll be too busy checking out the caravan to worry about where the call came from. Just be detailed, as if you were really there.'

'It feels like I was really there,' Will said. 'Alright, I'll do it. Wait here.'

As Will approached the payphone, he took a deep breath. He picked up the receiver and dialled 000.

The operator answered on the second ring. Will told her he wanted the New South Wales police. After a pause, the line connected, and a male voice spoke.

'Police, what's your emergency?'

Will bounced on his heels and tried to recreate the sense of panic he'd felt when he saw it all happen.

'Yeah, I'm a farmer in Stubbo, and I just drove past something pretty urgent.'

'What did you see, sir?'

'Two guys were running down a dirt road – Berry Drive. They were after a woman, and she looked really hurt. I drove down to get a better look, and saw them get into an old caravan. I would've missed it if I hadn't seen the two guys. It was covered in shrubbery, and pushed right back into the trees. I didn't want to go any further, because one had a gun, but the cops need to get down there quick.'

'Okay, sir. You said Berry Drive, Stubbo, correct?'

'Yes. Correct.'

'Can you describe the two men any further for me?'

Will closed his eyes and tried to remember what he'd seen.

'The bigger one was wearing a white singlet, and was covered in tattoos, all down both arms. The smaller guy was in black pants and a long-sleeved shirt.'

'What about the woman?'

'I couldn't see her properly, but when the two men caught up with her, they grabbed her and dragged her into the caravan.'

'And the firearm, sir?' the operator asked.

'A black pistol – definitely a handgun.'

'And what is your name?'

Will cleared his throat. 'Ah, I'm Eric Sanders. I run a sheep farm down the road.'

'Okay, Mr Sanders, we'll send some officers over there now.'

'Great,' Will replied. 'Just remember to tell them the caravan's down the dirt road, tucked into the left, near the first group of tall trees. It's easy to miss. Hell, I've lived here for years, and it was the first time I've seen it.'

'Sir, can I get your number, in case we need to contact you again?'

Will hesitated.

'Oh… just tell them who I am, all the local cops know me. I'll wait for them at the top of the road, anyway.'

'Alright, thank you. The police are on their way.'

EIGHTEEN

At 3 p.m. on a slow Saturday afternoon, Sergeant John Grady and Senior Constable Andrew Bently were enjoying a quiet coffee break. Grady, middle-aged and slightly overweight, sat with his feet on a desk, eating a biscuit, crumbs falling into his thick beard. Bently, the younger of the pair, with a clean-shaven head, sat upright, his long, thin hands cradling a warm mug. Gulgong Police Station, which more resembled an old red brick house than an actual government building, provided the usual perks of rural policing: chatting with locals and patrolling picturesque country scenes with very little criminal activity.

However, when an urgent call came over the radio, the pair quickly jumped to attention. Grady and Bently were two of only five officers assigned to the Gulgong station, who also patrolled the nearby town of Stubbo. They both knew Stubbo had a population of only a few hundred residents, entirely made up of farmers and their families.

'Two men, one with a gun, chasing a woman?' Bently said, repeating the call. 'Sounds like bullshit.'

'Don't forget throwing her in a caravan too,' Grady added.

'What do you make of it?' Bently asked, as he put his duty belt back on.

'Who knows. Let's just head down there and look around. Apparently, a local made the call – Eric Sanders. Heard of him?'

'Nope.'

'Me neither.'

Grady collected the car keys, and the two officers began the drive up the quiet highway toward Stubbo. En route, Bently logged into the car's dispatch computer and went through the details of the call again.

'Says here in the dispatch the caravan's pretty well hidden. Do you know Berry Drive at all?'

'Not really, so let's just keep our eyes open for anything suspicious,' Grady replied.

They arrived at Berry Drive five minutes later. Peering down the dusty dirt road, they couldn't see any farmhouses or sheds.

'The caller said he'd meet us here,' Bently said. 'I don't see him, though.'

Grady studied the thick bush ahead. 'This all seems pretty strange to me. Anyway, let's take a drive down there.'

The road was uneven, and the crunch of dirt beneath the tires was loud enough for anyone to hear them coming. Bently stuck his head out of the passenger window and searched for anything strange. As they rolled down the road, he got a glimpse of something shiny, buried in the trees.

'Stop the car,' he said.

Grady killed the engine.

'Look, through there.'

Thirty metres off the road, there was something large and metallic, covered in thick green shrubs. If Bently hadn't been trying his hardest to find something in the bushes, he would've easily missed it.

'Is that a caravan?' Grady asked.

'I don't know. Maybe, hard to say.' Bently squinted, trying to identify what he was looking at.

'Come on, let's go check it out.'

They left the car and made their way toward the covered object. As they neared, it became clear it was an old caravan with some serious rust damage. Carefully, they circled around it.

A male voice shouted, followed by a woman's scream. The officers looked at each other, and drew their guns, adrenaline racing through their bodies.

Grady signalled that he'd located the door, which faced away from the dirt road. They met at the door, and Grady whispered, 'It's going to be an outward-opening door, no use kicking at it. I'll wait here, you go back to the car and get the crowbar.'

'Got it.'

Returning with the steel crowbar, Bently said, 'I'll pry the door open as quickly as I can, then we go in hard and fast, yeah?

'Yes,' Grady said. 'Don't forget, the report mentioned a gun.'

Bently nodded. Carefully, he placed the tip of the crowbar into door, then pushed down hard. The flimsy caravan door flew open. Grady stormed the caravan and Bently quickly followed.

'Police, don't move!' both officers screamed, raising their guns.

When they saw what they were presented with, Grady and Bently felt their knees buckle. They kept their Glocks drawn on the two men inside the caravan while they tried to process the scene.

A young woman in pink pyjamas was tied to a wooden chair, covered in dirt, dried blood, and sweat. Knotted hair covered most of her face, and a dirty rag was stuffed in her mouth. The caravan itself was dark and dingy. The thin carpet was stained, and the meagre furniture was chipped and covered in spiderwebs. On a small round table was a gun, laptop and mobile phone.

The larger man moved quickly. He picked up the gun and tracked it toward them, but Grady reacted instantly and fired two shots directly into his chest. He collapsed, and the bound woman screamed. Bently kept his gun pointed at the smaller man, who trembled and raised his arms above his head.

'Don't you dare move!' Bently yelled.

Crouching by the larger man, Grady pried the small pistol from his hand and felt his neck. No pulse. Blood seeped from the two bullet wounds in his chest.

'Turn around, now,' Bently ordered the smaller man. 'No sudden movements.'

Grady made his way over to the woman. When he touched her arm, her body went into convulsions. She screamed and tried to shake him off.

'Hey, it's alright, I'm not going to hurt you,' Grady said. 'I'm a police officer, okay? I'm going to take this out of your mouth now.'

Slowly, he pulled the fabric down. The woman gasped and cried.

'Who are you?'

'Abby Sullivan,' she said. 'Get me out of here.'

***

Sergeant Yule raced through the halls of Surry Hills Police Station, rounding everyone into the conference room as quickly as he could. Woods, who was at her desk, working through her list of potential suspects, got up and followed.

Yule stood before the crowd, unable to contain a wide grin.

'Abby's been found. She's okay!'

The room erupted into cheers and applause. Moments earlier, every single person in that room had believed that Abby Sullivan's ransom would have to be paid.

'Alright, settle down. Here's the story. I just got off the phone with a detective from Mudgee, of all places. A witness called from Stubbo, a small town half an hour north of Mudgee, saying he'd seen a woman being chased. The locals found Abby in a beat-up old caravan hidden in the bush. One of the two men holding her was shot dead when he aimed a gun at the officers, but the other's in custody at Mudgee Police Station.'

As questions were thrown at Yule from all parts of the room, Woods sat dumbfounded, hearing more and more details of the exact scene Will Denham had described to her.

'Listen,' Yule continued. 'I want my team ready to head up to Mudgee in twenty minutes. Abby's been beaten up, but is otherwise okay. Woods, I want you to come along and stay with her in hospital while we arrange for Martin Sullivan to be transported there. She must be frightened, and she could use some support.'

Woods nodded.

'The two men haven't yet been identified, and the one in custody isn't talking, but we'll run their fingerprints to work out who they are.'

'What about the witness?' Woods called.

'We're still working on that. The caller identified himself as a local, but was nowhere to be found when police arrived. When they tried to find him for a statement, they actually traced the number back to a payphone in Sydney.'

Woods rubbed her chin. Lapis, who was sitting behind her, tapped her on the shoulder.

'You okay? I thought you'd be bouncing off the walls knowing they want you to go up with them.'

'Yeah, I'm fine. I'm glad Abby's safe.'

The more she thought about it, the more unsettled she felt about what Will had known, especially coupled with the anonymous call from Sydney. She even wondered if it was worth reporting to Yule, though in the end, she decided against it. The team had enough to worry about, and she wouldn't even know where to begin with such a crazy story.

'That's all for now, everyone – you're dismissed. Thank you for your hard work. I just want to talk to my team and Aubrey before we go.'

The room emptied, and Yule approached Woods.

'I want you to head off now. Drive straight to Mudgee Hospital and stay with Abby. I can only imagine how she must be feeling, but it's also important that we record anything she says. We'll arrange for a full statement when she gets discharged. For now, just keep her company and make her feel as safe as possible. My team and I will split between the police station and the crime scene. Call if you need anything,'

'Sure,' Woods said. She paused, still thinking about everything Will had told her.

'Everything okay?' Yule asked.

'Of course. I'll leave right away.'

Woods hurried out of the room, hoping it was the right decision to keep Will's information to herself.

NINETEEN

By the time Woods arrived at Mudgee Hospital, it was almost dark. The slow, winding drive through the Blue Mountains had allowed her time to think about Abby Sullivan and Will Denham. She knew Abby was safe at the hospital, but there was something strange about what Will had known.

Woods parked in front of the hospital and strode in via the emergency department. Flashing her badge at the nurse at the front counter, she asked to speak with Abby Sullivan's doctor. A short time later, the emergency room physician introduced himself to Woods. Dr Parker was an older man with thinning grey hair and round glasses. He looked fragile underneath his oversized lab coat, but greeted Woods with a firm handshake.

'How's she doing?' Woods asked.

'She's going to be okay. Physically, anyway. We'll keep her in tonight for observation.'

'Has she been talking much?'

'A little. She's obviously exhausted – I don't think she's slept much over the last few days. She gave us a brief account, though. Said two men took her from her bedroom, and she passed out after feeling a pinch in her neck. We expect they gave her some kind of sedative, but we're waiting on the toxicology results to confirm. They then drove her to a warehouse, and—'

'Sorry, did you say a warehouse?' Woods interrupted.

'Yes, well, that's what she told us. We didn't probe for specifics, we just needed to know enough to treat her. She said they drove her to the caravan later, and while there, was physically assaulted and tied up. They gave her a small amount of food and water, but not nearly enough, so we have her on a drip. I expect she'll recount the full version to you when she's ready.'

'Okay, when can I see her?'

'Now, if you like. She's awake. A little sore, but you can talk to her.'

Woods followed him down a long, sterile hallway. The hospital was quiet, with hardly any staff working – a vast difference to what she was used to in the city.

'It's the last door on the left there.'

'Thank you, Doctor.'

'Please take it slowly with her. I don't have to tell you she's been through a lot.'

Woods nodded. Approaching the open door, she knocked gently on the side wall. She'd seen several photographs of Abby, but tonight, she was looking at a different person. Abby's face was swollen and bruised, her hair was matted, and there was no smile on her face, unlike the happy portraits scattered throughout the Sullivan residence.

'Hi, Abby. I'm Aubrey Woods, a detective from the Sydney police.'

'Where's Martin? Does he know I'm here? Is he okay?'

'Yes, he's alright, and happy you're safe. We all are. Another detective is going to bring him here soon.'

Abby didn't respond, but relief was written all over her face.

'How are you feeling?' Woods asked.

'A bit sore,' Abby said, as she touched her face and started crying.

'Hey, it's okay. Everything's okay now.'

'Every time I close my eyes, I see them,' Abby sobbed.

'I'm so sorry this happened to you, I really am. We'll do everything we can to get the help you need.'

Woods sat on a chair beside Abby's bed.

'Why did they take me?'

'It looks like they knew of Martin's success with his work in cryptocurrency and wanted him to pay for your release, but there's a lot we don't know yet. What I can promise you is they will not hurt you again.'

Abby buried her head in her hands and continued to sob. Woods sat in silence for a moment, and thought about everything she'd heard during the day. From Will Denham, from Ian Yule, from Dr Parker. She took out her notepad and a pen.

'Abby, I don't want to take a full statement from you tonight, but can I ask some brief questions? It might really help.'

Abby nodded.

'What do you remember about the night you were taken?'

'Not much,' she said. 'I was sleeping, but I heard noise, and saw Martin was being attacked. The next thing I knew, a man grabbed me, and...'

She paused, wiping away fresh tears.

'Maybe we'll come back to that part later,' Woods said, and placed a hand atop hers. 'Do you remember where they took you?'

'I passed out, and woke up tied to a chair in some warehouse. After that, they drove me to the caravan. I didn't even know where I was until the paramedics told me.'

'What type of warehouse was it?'

'I don't know, it was big and empty. That's where they held me while they called Martin. Next thing I knew, I was thrown in the back of a car, and we drove for hours. I managed to untie myself.

When they stopped, I tried to get away. I kicked the big one and ran, but they caught me.'

Abby looked up at Woods, her eyes red and wet.

'They told me they were going to kill me because I saw their faces,' she said, and broke down again.

'Okay, I think that's enough for now. Can I get you anything? Are you thirsty?'

Abby shook her head and sunk into her pillow, sobbing. Woods considered everything she'd said, before leaning in close.

'Do you know a person called Will Denham?'

'No. Is he one of the people who took me?'

'He's not. It's nothing, forget it.' Woods sat back in her chair and let Abby rest.

An hour later, Martin Sullivan rushed into the room, followed by Sergeant Yule. At the first sight of Abby, Martin broke down in tears and climbed on the bed, hugging her tightly. Yule nodded at Woods, and they left the room to give the pair some privacy.

'The doctor says she's going to be okay,' Yule said.

'She's a very strong woman.'

'Some of my guys are speaking with our kidnapper.' Yule took a chair in the hallway and invited Woods to sit next to him. 'He's refusing to identify himself, but is claiming it was a plan the dead guy made after learning of Martin's cryptocurrency wealth, and that he was coerced to go along with it. No one's buying that. It's easy to blame everything on the guy who can't defend himself, but it won't hold up in court.'

'When Abby's ready to give a full statement, she'll tell us how it really was,' Woods said.

'Absolutely. Somehow I suspect the guy back at the station wasn't just along for the ride. Either way, he isn't going anywhere. We've also identified the deceased – his name was Chris Pollard, an organised crime standover man.'

'That's good news,' Woods said, yawning.

'Look, I know it's been a long day, but would you mind staying here a few more hours to make sure they're okay? Then find a hotel, get some sleep. We'll have a meeting at Mudgee Police Station tomorrow morning, then you might as well head back to Sydney.'

'Oh, I was hoping to stay on this one,' Woods said, disappointed.

'I know, but we've got it covered. It's open and shut now,' Yule said. 'I heard from your supervisor that you're interested in working with us, and there'll be an opening on my team soon. I'm keeping you in mind.'

'Thanks, I appreciate that.'

By midnight, both Sullivans were asleep. It was probably the first time in days that either of them had rested safe and soundly. Woods smiled and went to check into her motel.

The next morning, she woke early from a horrible sleep in an old musty room. After grabbing a takeaway coffee, she was the first to arrive at Mudgee Police Station. The rest of the team must've worked well into the night. As she made her way around the back of the station, searching for the detective's office, she found a tall, rugged John Wayne look-alike walking out of a small kitchen with a cup of coffee. He wore a baggy grey suit, a thick blue tie, and dusty leather boots.

'Hi, I'm Aubrey Woods from Sydney,' she said, offering her hand. 'Just here working on the kidnapping.'

'G'day. Brad Murphy,' he said, in a deep, croaky voice, and they shook hands.

'Were you on the scene yesterday?'

'Yeah, got there after the locals from Gulgong called it in. Come on, I'll show you to the detectives' office.' Murphy led her to a small room, filled with six desks and three detectives. They all gave Woods a nod and smile, before returning to their work.

'It's not much, but there are only six of us in the entire region,' Murphy said. 'We don't get a huge amount of crime out here. Take a seat, make yourself comfortable.'

'Thanks,' said Woods, as she sat behind a spare computer. 'How are the officers involved in the shooting? Must be hard for them right now.'

'They're alright. They're both tough guys, and they had no choice but to shoot. It was him or them.'

Woods nodded. They'd done their job well, though the act of taking a life, no matter how justified, must've still taken its toll.

'How'd you go locating the witness?' she asked.

'No luck, I'm afraid. He wasn't there when we showed up, and the name he gave... what was it?' Murphy rummaged through paperwork on his desk. 'Ah, Eric Sanders. He's supposed to be a local, but no one around here has heard of him. Pretty weird.'

'I heard the call actually came from Sydney.'

'Correct. A payphone, too. I guess it doesn't matter – we caught the perps red-handed, and the woman's safe.'

'I guess,' Woods said. 'You wouldn't have a copy of the call, would you?'

'Yeah, here. They emailed the file to us yesterday.' Murphy handed Woods a small thumb drive. 'Log on to a free computer and have a listen.'

Murphy returned to his desk, and Woods opened the file. It took her all of half a second to realise the caller's voice was Will Denham's. She listened to the entire call, and was stunned by how clearly he'd described the scene. When she'd finished, she removed the USB and handed it back to Murphy.

'I'm just going to go for a walk, enjoy the fresh Mudgee air.'

'You alright?' he asked. 'You look a little rattled.'

'Yeah, fine. Cheers.'

Woods found a bench in a quiet park, where she finished her coffee and thought about Will. Nothing about him made sense. How had he known so much? Tony Hartley and the fire, the warehouse, and now the caravan… it was too much to process so early in the morning. Coupled with her poor night's sleep, she felt drained and confused.

A short time later, Yule and his team arrived at the Mudgee Police Station. Woods joined them at the doors, and followed them back to the detectives' office. Yule gathered his team and the locals together.

'The good news is, we've identified our second offender using facial recognition, and found his driver's licence on file.' Yule consulted his notepad. 'Name is Donald Evans. No criminal record, and he works a steady finance job in the Sydney CBD.'

Lowering his notes, Yule cleared his throat. 'He's been charged and refused bail. We don't know how he came to be involved, but as we review the phone and computer recovered from the caravan, I'm sure we'll work it out. We've already connected the phone to the ransom call received by Martin Sullivan, and located software that would've been used to mask the caller's voice.'

His craggy face broke into a smile. 'Now to even better news – Abby Sullivan's being released any minute now, and she'll be going home.'

The room filled with applause and handshakes, as everyone congratulated each other on an amazing result. Yet Woods knew that if it weren't for Will Denham's call, Abby Sullivan would likely have been dead.

*

All night, Will tossed and turned, trying to imagine how his anonymous call was being treated by the police. What if it wasn't taken seriously, or they figured out he wasn't an actual witness?

Even if everything went well, there was probably no way for him to find out the result. He didn't know any of the local police, and Woods was refusing to speak to him.

Pulling himself out of bed, he made himself a cup of tea. As he glanced over at the computer in the corner of his living room, what Ravi had said yesterday about basic precognition came back to him.

Will realised his previous approach to researching his condition had been all wrong. When he'd searched several days earlier, the results were related to hallucinations, and all came back to schizophrenia and other mental disorders. However, Will knew he was healthy.

Switching on the computer, he began researching precognition, anticipatory timing, and the rhythmic patterns of the brain. On one forum, a man from South Australia described an experience he'd had while surfing at a popular beach. As he'd been paddling out to catch his first wave of the day, he'd had a feeling something wasn't right. He hadn't been able to explain it, but had just felt he shouldn't be in the water. He'd quickly paddled into shore. That evening, on the news, he'd heard another surfer had been attacked by a great white shark at the same beach, about 30 minutes after he'd left.

While Will couldn't find anyone on the forums who'd had an experience like his, he read some well-researched articles by forward-thinking scholars that emphasised how much the scientific community still had to learn about the human brain. Although people were so quick to discount things they didn't fully understand, legitimate medical and scientific research was still discovering new things the brain could do. On the downside, given the lack of knowledge about the brain's potential, he thought it unlikely he'd ever find out more about his visions.

As Will became increasingly wrapped up in his research, the day quickly got away from him. Just after 6 p.m., Ravi called.

'Hey, Ravi.'

'Quick – Channel Nine, now!'

Will hurried to grab the remote from the couch and switch the TV on. The broadcast had just started covering the rescue of a kidnapping victim in Stubbo.

'Are you seeing this?'

Will was frozen, staring at the TV.

'Yeah, I'll ring you back,' Ravi said, and ended the call.

Will sat down without removing his eyes from the news story. A reporter wearing a suit and tie stood in front of the same beaten-up caravan Will had seen, which was marked with crime scene tape and surrounded by police taking photographs and bagging evidence.

'In the caravan just behind me, Abby Sullivan was detained while her two kidnappers waited for the payment of her million-dollar ransom,' the reporter began. 'Mrs Sullivan, wife of successful cryptocurrency entrepreneur Martin Sullivan, was taken in a violent invasion from her Paddington home late on Thursday night. Police immediately began an investigation, while withholding any information from the media, given the dangerous situation Mrs Sullivan faced.'

The reporter gestured to the rusted caravan. 'Yesterday, police discovered two men holding Mrs Sullivan here at gunpoint. One challenged police with a firearm and was fatally shot. The other remains in custody, and has since been charged with Mrs Sullivan's kidnapping. Earlier today, he fronted court, where he was formally refused bail.'

The scene cut to a solemn-faced man with thick red hair. Beneath him was a line of text: Detective Chief Inspector Munro of the Robbery and Serious Crime Squad.

'Thanks to an anonymous tip, we successfully located where Mrs Sullivan was being held hostage,' Munro said. 'With the fine work of the local police, we were able to prevent any ransom from being paid, and safely retrieve Mrs Sullivan.'

By the end of the report, Will was standing with his attention fixed on every word.

He'd done it. The woman had been saved.

TWENTY

Ravi was waiting on the street before a corner pub. After Will had called him back, they'd decided to go out drinking to celebrate and unwind. When he saw Will approach, he tapped on his wristwatch.

'Yeah, I know,' Will said. 'I'm sorry. I lost track of time reading about what happened.'

'All good. I thought maybe you were... you know, seeing something.' Ravi laughed.

Will smiled back. 'Let's get inside. It's cold.'

Entering the old pub, they went upstairs to the balcony beer garden. It was lit up with hundreds of tiny fairy lights, and busy with several large groups, but they found a small table overlooking the street. Ravi went to the bar and bought a couple of beers.

'Cheers,' said Ravi, and they both took a long drink. 'So, how're you feeling?'

'Okay, I guess. I was doing my best to make sense of it all, but I had no idea I was seeing a live kidnapping. I even read a news article about the kidnapper's court appearance. Apparently, Abby Sullivan was going to be killed regardless of whether a ransom was paid.'

'So that woman would've died without your help?' Ravi said.

'I guess. And that's why I'm still feeling a bit off. I mean, I'm relieved, and happy she's alright, but... I don't know.'

'What do you mean?' Ravi took another sip.

'Well, what if I hadn't seen it? What if I'd ignored what I saw, or never called it in?' Will shook his head, leg bouncing. 'She'd be dead. And what if I keep seeing people in trouble? All that responsibility, but no one to believe me. I can't go from payphone to payphone making crazy police reports – they'll catch on to that.'

He dropped his head into his hands.

'I'm spending every minute in anticipation of seeing something new. It's exhausting.'

For the first time since his earliest vision in the bathroom, Will felt they were out of his control, and dreaded having to deal with more of them. Both series of visions had turned into something real and horrific, and that frightened him. It was not a game.

'Will, if it weren't for you, that woman would be dead. Focus on that. You saved someone's life.'

Will rubbed his tired eyes and took a long drink, as Ravi continued.

'I don't know why this is happening, or if it'll ever happen again, but you don't have to be alone through it all.'

Will watched pedestrians hurry down the dark street below.

'The first time I saw something,' he said, 'I was terrified. Then the second lot of visions happened, and I felt a strange addiction to them. I wanted to see more. But now... I don't know. Someone could've died today.'

'But they didn't,' Ravi replied. 'Because of you.'

Will looked back to Ravi, who met his gaze earnestly.

'I guess,' Will said. 'Thanks for the support. It's just scary, you know?'

'No, I don't know. I can't even imagine what it's like, but I still think it's amazing.'

'How's your research on all this going?' Will asked.

'Not great. Nothing like it has ever been documented before.' Ravi sighed, running a finger around the rim of his glass. 'The thing is, we barely understand the brain of an earthworm, let alone a human. With no precedent, I'm not sure I'll find anything helpful.'

They finished their beers. Ravi insisted on buying another round, and left for the bar while the line wasn't too long.

The phone inside Will's pocket began vibrating. Pulling it out, he saw the caller ID was a familiar number.

'Will, it's Aubrey Woods.'

After a brief silence, Will said, 'I didn't think I'd ever hear from you again.'

'I just want to know what's going on,' Woods said, her tone much softer than the last time they'd spoken.

'What do you mean?'

'I know you made the call about the kidnapping victim. I heard it myself.'

Will glanced around the pub to make sure nobody was close enough to overhear.

'Everything I told you happened, didn't it?' he asked.

'Seriously, who are you? Nothing about this makes sense.'

'I know, but ever since the night I was assaulted, I've been seeing things – the fire at the store, and now this.'

'Well, Abby's alive because of the call you made. I just got back from Mudgee, and I've been thinking about what you've said to me over the past few days.'

Will didn't reply. Woods sighed.

'What I'm trying to say is… I'm sorry for not believing you, but I hope you understand how crazy you sounded. It still sounds crazy. Look, I have the day off tomorrow. Can we meet up and chat about it?'

'Sure, but not as a cop thing. No interrogations. And don't tell anyone too much, okay? I don't want to end up in a lab with probes in my brain.'

'Just us, I promise. Say 10 a.m. tomorrow, Brown and Blondes cafe at Surry Hills?'

'I'll see you then.'

Will put his phone away as Ravi returned with the fresh beers.

'You won't believe who I just spoke to,' he said.

***

The next morning, Will arrived at the cafe right on time. As he neared the entrance, he saw Woods sitting alone at a table facing out onto the street. She looked different to the past occasions he'd seen her. She wore denim jeans and a white cardigan, and her long blonde hair was down, glowing in the daylight. Will suddenly felt underdressed in his baggy tracksuit pants and hoodie. Seeing him through the window, she waved him inside.

He sat down opposite her. It felt like an awkward first date, and he had no idea how to break the ice. Luckily, the waitress came over to take their orders. After she'd left, Woods spoke first.

'Thanks for meeting with me. I'm here as a regular person, not as a cop. After everything that's happened, I just need to know what's going on.' She tilted her head, framed against the cafe's bustling front counter. 'You look better, by the way,' she added. 'Your face is healing well.'

They stared at each other as Will thought about how to begin. He couldn't help but think Woods transitioned from cop to civilian pretty seamlessly. Reminding himself that she'd invited him to talk about it, he just came out with it directly.

'I've been having visions.'

Woods nodded.

Encouraged by this, Will detailed his visions, from the fire at Tony's Convenience to the screams of Abby Sullivan.

The waitress brought over their coffee, and they both took a long sip.

'So, do you have any idea what's causing them?' Woods asked.

'Here's what I think.' Will pushed his coffee to the side and leaned over the table, keeping his voice low. 'People have always just accepted certain limitations, keeping to what's considered normal. Anything they don't understand, or science doesn't support, they consider crazy talk. But science can't explain everything. Just look at some of the remarkable things people have done.'

Will paused, sitting back in his seat as the waitress brought over their food. He continued when she was out of earshot.

'You might think we have five senses, but from all I've read, we have loads more. Like that feeling you get when something just isn't right – that something bad is going to happen.'

'I'm with you. Keep going.'

'I'm thinking my assault triggered a different sense. It unlocked something in my mind, and now I can see and feel things people can't explain.' Sighing, he sat back in his chair. 'I'm just trying to understand it as best I can.'

'A few weeks ago, I couldn't have imagined I'd speak to someone who claims to be having visions,' Woods said. 'I would've thought I was going crazy. But I can't ignore everything you've said. Honestly, we never would've found Abby without you.'

Will took a few bites of his food, while Woods drained her coffee and ordered another.

Eventually, she broke the silence.

'So, what's it like? Describe it to me.'

'The visions?'

'Yeah.'

'Well, they're pretty strange, like a full sensory overload, and very spontaneous... there was actually a little incident when I went to the victim support group you told me about.' Will squirmed at the memory.

'What happened?'

'Well, it was only my second vision, so I didn't know what was going on. I saw a building on fire across the street, and sprinted out of the meeting to help. Two people tried to drag me back inside. There was no fire. They thought I was insane, so I kind of ran away.' Will slumped deeper into his chair, remembering the embarrassment he'd felt.

'If it's any consolation, I've seen people have worse psychiatric episodes at those meetings. I'm sure Sarah just wanted to make sure you were okay.'

'Still, I probably gave everyone a good fright – or at least an interesting story to tell.'

The waitress returned with Woods's second coffee and cleared the plates away. Will waited for her to leave, then lowered his voice.

'At the meeting, Sarah told me you were hurt pretty bad once.'

Woods put her cup down, her expression turning gloomy.

'Sorry, that was rude of me,' Will said.

'No, it's fine,' she said. 'You've told me your story, it's only fair I tell mine.'

She looked out of the window and sighed.

'I was three years into the job,' she began. 'Still in uniform, just waiting for a spot in the detectives' office to open up. My partner and I responded to a routine call one Saturday night. A noise complaint about a house party. We got there, banged on the door, and asked them to turn the music down. They were all drunk, and the entire group just suddenly turned on us. It was two against at least forty. We tried to wave our batons, use our capsicum spray, but we were outnumbered.' Woods paused, exhaled, and took another sip of coffee, before continuing her recount.

'It only took about three minutes for our backup to arrive, but it was the longest three minutes of my life. My partner got a glass bottle smashed across his face, and I got stabbed. Right in my stomach. With a pocketknife, I was later told.'

She placed a hand on her belly.

'I collapsed, but luckily backup had arrived, and stopped them from doing anything worse. I was rushed to St Vincent's Hospital on the other side of the city. If City South had been built by then, I would've been far better off.' She grimaced. 'The blade ruptured my spleen. I stayed in hospital for over a week. My partner had several operations to fix his face, but it was never the same, and neither was he. He resigned from the police. I nearly did too, but this job is all I have, aside from my family.'

'What happened to the people who attacked you?'

'Well, the riot squad came and broke the crowd up. Most of them ran away, but my attacker and my partner's attacker were arrested.'

'And you eventually went back to work?'

'Yes, after about two months. I never wore a uniform again, though. I went on restricted duties, working intelligence, before I got my transfer to the detective squad. Now, I've been there for five years.'

'Do you ever get scared that something bad will happen again?' Will asked, remembering his own attack.

'Yeah, I do. I think about it a lot, but I've been going to therapy, and the group sessions at the church. Both my parents were cops, so it's all I've ever wanted to do. It's all I know, and all I've got.'

They both sat quietly for a moment, finishing their coffee.

'With my attack… I always wanted to know why,' Will said. 'Did you ever get any sort of closure?'

'Nope, not even an apology. I just had to move on, without living in fear. Otherwise they'd win. There's no point hiding from it, and that's why I go to the victim group as often as I can.'

'I don't think I'll go back there after what happened.'

'I hope you reconsider. It really is a safe place, I promise.'

Woods checked the time, then grabbed her handbag.

'I'd better get going, but thank you for everything, Will. I'm truly glad you called the kidnapping in. If we'd found her body at the place you described after I'd ignored you, I never would've forgiven myself. I'm paying for breakfast – no arguments.'

'Thanks, Aubrey. I'll have to get the next one, then.'

'Sounds good. Don't be a stranger. You know where to find me.'

After Woods left, Will sat at the table for a moment longer.

Now, he had two people whom he could confide in. He wasn't alone anymore.

TWENTY-ONE

The following Monday morning, Will stared at the grey shirt and matching pants laid out on his bed. Looking at the hospital uniform, he was reminded of the last time he'd worn it. His old set had probably been incinerated. Although he felt some hesitation about returning to work, he remembered what Woods had told him about not living in fear. With all he'd been through in the last week, he felt like a completely different person with a whole new sense of confidence.

An hour later, Will reported for work. He was pleased to find the rest of the maintenance team had kept up their usual fine standard, so there wasn't much for him to do. He spent the better part of the morning roaming around the hospital, receiving good wishes from the staff, many of whom were speaking with him for the first time.

As he made his way through the emergency department, a nurse in light pink scrubs waved him down.

'Hey there. Do you have a moment?' they asked. 'I just went to grab some stuff from ER storage, and a pipe was dripping water all over the floor.'

'Sure, I'll look at it.'

As had been described, Will found water seeping from a copper pipe running across the ceiling of the storage room. He used a small stepladder and quickly repaired the leak by tightening the joint. As he got down, his knees buckled, vision blurring. He caught himself on a shelf and shook his head. Slowly, his vision returned.

The medical supplies were gone. Now, the shelves surrounding him contained hundreds of strange metal canisters, each wrapped in coloured wires.

Will slowed his breathing and tried to calm his mind. He knew it had to be a premonition, but his heart was racing. Picking up one of the pipes, he was surprised at how heavy and cold it was. He turned it over and nearly dropped it when he saw a digital timer stuck to its back. The display was blank, as though it wasn't activated. Carefully, he returned it to the shelf.

As he continued to sort through the heavy canisters, finding them all identical to the first, smoke flooded into the room, filling his lungs. He gasped for air. A sudden ringing pierced his ears, and he fell to his knees, clawing at his head.

The sound cut out. The smoke cleared, and the room returned to normal. The pipe canisters had vanished. The supplies took their usual places on the shelves. Will stumbled into the corridor, coughing up the last bit of smoke he'd inhaled. A nurse ran over to him.

'Are you okay? Are you choking?' she asked, patting his back.

'I'm fine,' Will replied. He glanced back at the storage room, which was still completely normal. The nurse followed his gaze.

'Is everything okay in there?' she asked.

'Yeah, all good. There was a leak I was fixing, but I'm fine, really,' he said, trying to force a smile.

'Well, alright. Take it easy.'

After she'd left, Will pulled out his phone and called Ravi.

'Hey, it happened again just now!'

'What do you mean? You're back at work, right? You had a vision at the hospital?'

'Yes – meet me by the incinerator room in five minutes, it'll be quiet there. I'll fill you in.'

Quickly, Will dropped the ladder off at the maintenance office, before jogging to meet Ravi. He arrived first, and waited behind the metal dumpster next to the incinerator room.

A moment later, Ravi came charging around the corner.

'What did you see?'

'I was in a medical storage room, fixing a leaking pipe,' Will said. 'My vision went all strange, and next thing I knew, I was surrounded by these small metal canisters. I think they were bombs. You know, like pipe bombs from the movies, with little timers on—'

The high-pitched ringing returned, screeching through his skull, even more intense than before. He fell to his knees, covering his ears and clenching his teeth. Ravi's face appeared before him, his mouth moving, but his voice was drowned out by the ringing.

As suddenly as the noise had started, it stopped.

'I heard that in the storage room too,' Will said, stretching his jaw and tugging on his ears.

'Heard what? Are you okay?'

'This ringing noise. It started just after the room filled with thick smoke... I thought I was going to cough up a lung.'

'These are some serious physical reactions to something happening in your mind.'

Will shrugged. 'Don't know what to tell you.'

'Let's get you back to the MRI scanner. I want to see whether there's any change after a fresh vision, if you're up for it?'

'Yeah, I'm okay.'

'What else did you see?'

'That's it,' Will said. 'I was trying to find out what it all meant, but that's all I saw.'

'I'm sure you'll work it out,' Ravi said. 'You did with all the others.'

Shortly after, Will found himself back in that white magnetic tube. The lights flashed on, and he wriggled as he tried to adjust his eyes.

'Keep your eyes closed, and remember to stay still. It won't take long,' Ravi said, through the microphone in the adjacent room.

Will tried his best to remain motionless. Fifteen minutes later, Ravi rejoined him.

'Completely clear,' Ravi said. 'Nothing abnormal showed up at all, and I've listened to your chest. No signs of smoke inhalation.'

'What do you make of that?'

'Same as last time. Whatever's going on is only inside your head, and even if there is some extra brain activity, it might only change during an actual vision.'

'I think I'm going to call the detective. She's on board now, and maybe she can make some sense of it.'

'Tell me if anything else happens, okay?'

Ravi walked back toward the psych unit, and Will made his way to the back end of the hospital, where he knew it would be quiet.

'Detective Aubrey Woods,' she answered.

'Hey, it's Will – I've just had another vision.'

'Hang on a sec.'

Will heard a door shut, cutting off the chatter in the background.

'What did you see?' Woods asked.

'Not much, so I'm hoping you can help me figure it out. When I was at the hospital, I saw a bunch of what I think were homemade bombs.'

'Are you sure that's what they were?'

'Well, I don't know. My only experience with bombs is from the movies.'

'Mine too, if I'm being honest.'

Will ran through his entire premonition, including the smoke and the piercing ringing. Woods listened to every detail intently.

'What do you make of it?' he asked.

'I don't like this. Given your track record of… well, let's say accuracy – it's worrying if you actually saw bombs, but I don't know what I can do about it.'

'Isn't there anyone you can call?'

'Yes, but that's not the problem. There just isn't enough detail. We don't know when or where these might appear. You definitely didn't see anything else?'

'I didn't, sorry.'

'Let me know if you find out more, and I'll look into it right away.'

'I will. I know it isn't much to go on, but I needed to tell you.'

That evening, Will left the hospital via the emergency department, as he'd always done. The sun was on its way down, but he still had a bit of light to make his way home. He couldn't help remembering what'd happened the last time he'd walked back from work, but Woods's mantra about not living in fear held him in good stead as he rounded the corner where the attack had taken place. A man was raking up leaves out the front of his house, and stopped when he saw Will.

'Hi there,' he called out. Will flinched. 'You probably don't remember me, but I was there when… well, when you got attacked. How are you feeling?'

'Of course, I'm sorry I didn't recognise you,' Will replied, relieved. 'Yeah, I'm healing up well. Thank you for what you did.'

'Don't sweat it – we all have to look out for each other. I'm glad you're doing okay.'

As Will continued on his way home, he decided he wouldn't let what'd happened hold him back anymore. After everything he'd seen and done, he couldn't afford to be afraid.

TWENTY-TWO

Will woke violently to a deep rumbling. As the bed shook, he gripped the headboard and tried to ride it out, assuming he was caught in an earthquake – though he hadn't ever heard of one occurring in inner Sydney.

The vibrations crawled through his entire body. His head ached. His bedroom TV turned itself on at full volume, flashing images of explosions and collapsing buildings. Panting and covered in sweat, he searched for the remote, finding it tucked between his sheets. He pointed it at the TV. Nothing happened. Frantically, he began pressing every button on the remote, but scenes of destruction continued to burst across the screen.

Will scrambled for the power point in the corner of the room and yanked out the plug. The TV stayed on. He slapped its side and tore the cords from its back until the screen flicked out. The room went black, and he felt his way back to bed. Lying down, he stared at the ceiling, hearing nothing but his own heavy breaths. As he closed his eyes and tried to fall asleep again, the high-pitched ringing returned.

He clutched at his ears. Nothing helped. The ringing continued, and the room spun. His eyes closed forcefully, and a blinding white light surrounded him, followed by images of enormous explosions, one after the other. Will tried to open his eyes, but his body was frozen.

He stood before the main entrance to City South. Looking around, he saw all the familiar features of the hospital, from the cobblestone path to the garden wrapped around the building.

The doors slid open. Will's legs carried him through. Inside, the hospital was no longer as he'd known it.

It had been annihilated. The walls and ceilings had collapsed, dust filled the air, and the floor was strewn with debris. Turning back, he saw the entrance was now a pile of rubble. He made his way deeper into the hospital, exploring the wreckage. Bright sunlight poured straight into what was left of the emergency room, but as the ringing in his ears continued, he found it difficult to see.

In the general ward, he found several figures littered across the floor. Wiring sparked and soot swirled as he walked through a field of bodies.

Doctors, nurses, patients and visitors filled the destroyed room. Most were facedown or partially hidden under fallen debris, their clothing burnt and torn. There were no signs of life. A wave of dust swept over Will, and he gasped for air. As his lungs became painfully filled, his eyes snapped open, and he exhaled back in his dark bedroom.

Panting and horrified, Will reached to check his phone. 1:45 a.m. He slowly lifted himself from his bed and headed for the bathroom. After splashing his face with cool water, he ran back to his phone.

He'd now experienced two visions in less than 24 hours. They had to be linked.

After at least fifteen rings, Woods picked up her phone.

'Hello,' she said sleepily.

'Sorry, I know it's early, but it happened again. I saw explosions at City South Hospital, and I don't think we have much time,' he said, so urgently it sounded like one long word.

'Huh? Will, it's one in the morning. What're you talking about?'

'I saw the hospital destroyed. The roof had caved in, and there were bodies everywhere.'

'When did it happen?' Woods asked, suddenly more alert.

'It was daytime,' Will said. 'I can't take a risk with this one. What if it's today?'

'Can we evacuate the hospital?'

'Yeah, but for how long, and what do we say? We can't keep people out forever.'

'Meet me there in the morning. I start work at seven, and I'll go straight over. I'll tell my boss I have to pick up some records for a case – best not to create alarm just yet.'

Will put down his phone. He was wide awake and scared, and he spent the next four hours tossing and turning.

He arrived at the hospital early, just after sunup. Prior to leaving, he'd texted Ravi, asking him to meet out the front. When Ravi arrived, Will told him everything he'd seen last night, and confirmed with absolute certainty that the hospital he'd walked through was City South.

'So, you're saying you don't know when it happened? It could be at any time?' Ravi asked, sounding as anxious as anyone would under the circumstances.

'I think I've actually seen all this before, and not just in the storage room yesterday,' Will replied.

'What do you mean?'

'When I was here after the assault, I had these recurring dreams where I was wandering through the hospital, and the whole place was wrecked.'

'You think they were about the same incident?'

'I mean, they were dreams. I remember actually waking up after each of them, so they weren't like my other visions... but still, it can't just be a coincidence.'

Woods arrived a few minutes past 7 a.m. After Will introduced her to Ravi, they both looked expectantly at Will.

'What I've told you both is all I know,' he said. 'I wish I had something more specific to add, but we'll have to work with what we've got.'

'So, is evacuating the hospital our best option?' Ravi asked.

Woods shook her head. 'I didn't think about this when Will first called me, but if there's something or someone inside, an evacuation could make them panic and detonate early.'

'We have to assume that it could happen at any time,' Will said. 'That's why I wanted to talk to you both. But we have to keep it quiet for now – we could cause mass panic, or people might just assume I'm crazy. Either way, not an ideal outcome.'

'Could someone actually have access to explosives in Sydney?' Ravi asked.

'It's possible,' Woods said. 'There's plenty of information on the internet. Someone with the determination and know-how could make something after a bit of research.' She peered up at the hospital. 'How could someone from the public gain access to the building?'

'It wouldn't be hard, really,' Ravi said. 'The staff's too busy to notice people coming and going, and the place is huge.'

'They could work here,' Will said.

'Surely not.'

'We need to be open to anything,' Woods said. 'Can you think of anyone who'd do this?'

'No,' replied Will.

Ravi shrugged. 'But who really knows. Hundreds of people work here.'

'Let's split up and start searching, but be discreet,' Will said. 'Fingers crossed we find nothing. I truly hope I'm wrong.'

Woods nodded. 'If you do see something, do not touch it. Call me immediately.'

'Got it,' replied both Will and Ravi.

All three entered through the emergency door. Will felt sick at the thought of walking into a building that was potentially lined with explosives, but there were thousands of people inside, who he wasn't prepared to abandon.

Ravi left to search the psychiatric ward, while Woods remained in the Intensive Care Unit. On any ordinary day, police came and went for a range of reasons, so she wouldn't look out of place. Will had the luxury of being granted uninterrupted access to any part of the hospital. He went by the empty surgical theatres, which would be used later in the day, before fetching a ladder and checking the roof cavities in the emergency room.

After nearly thirty minutes of searching with no signs of anything suspicious, Will remembered the storage room from his vision yesterday. He hurried straight there. Arriving at the door, he took a deep breath, slid his skeleton key into the lock, and carefully opened it.

Nothing. Everything was as it should be, each shelf stocked with the usual supplies. He slammed the door shut, and took out his phone to see how the others were going. While he waited for Woods to pick up, he stared blankly into the distance. Behind an unattended nurse's station was an old analogue clock. It was the kind of cheap-looking, mass-produced clock they had scattered around the hospital. The hands told him it was 7:45 a.m.

As the line continued to ring, the hands began to speed up, until they were spinning around the face. They stopped at the exact hour of 9 a.m. Will's eyes were fixated on the clock.

'Will? Will, are you there?' Woods asked.

The clock's second hand began jerking backwards, with a loud, slow ticking sound.

He blinked. The clock returned to the current time, 7:46 a.m.

'I saw something,' he said.

'What?'

'A clock. The time changed.'

'Oh.' Woods sounded deflated.

'No, listen – the clock hands moved. They spun around and pointed to 9 a.m., then the second hand started going counterclockwise, and I heard a clicking sound. Like a countdown.'

'Nine? That's just over an hour from now.'

'An hour and fourteen minutes,' Will said. 'Where are you now?'

'Still in the ICU.'

'I'll call Ravi. Meet me outside the emergency ward, and hurry.'

Both Woods and Ravi arrived within a minute. Their troubled expressions matched Will's.

'I think something will happen at nine a.m. today,' Will said.

'I have an idea,' Woods said.

'Go on.'

'Ravi, where are the fire alarms?'

'All over, they're on every floor,' he said, looking confused. 'I thought we decided we weren't going to set off the alarm?'

'Well, I hope we don't have to,' replied Woods. 'How long would it take to evacuate the hospital?'

'It can take hours, even when we aren't at full capacity.'

'Damn.' Woods scowled. 'Well, we won't have that much time.'

'There's a good evacuation plan,' Will said. 'And we have fireproof areas. Maybe some people could go to them temporarily.'

Woods sighed deeply, before moving closer to Will and Ravi

and lowering her voice. 'Listen, we just have to do our best in the short time we have. But if there's a bomb, we need to find it. Otherwise, people are going to get hurt no matter what we do.'

Will had nothing to say. He knew she was right – the hospital was simply too big.

'I know it isn't ideal, but we have to minimise casualties, okay? It's hard to think like that, but every life saved is a win.'

Will nodded, and Ravi reluctantly agreed.

'Good,' she said. 'Keep searching. There are still parts of the outer perimeter I want to check, and you two should also start looking outside. Be fast but thorough. Ravi, if you don't hear from us earlier, pull the fire alarm ten minutes before nine and get as many people out as you can. Scream that there's a raging fire if it helps move them faster.'

'What if an actual bomber is here, and the alarm makes them set it off earlier?' Ravi asked.

'That's why I'm leaving it to the last minute – so we have the best chance of finding it first,' Woods said. 'Anyway, if it gets to that stage and if Will was right about the time of detonation, it won't make a difference. It's far from a perfect plan, but it's all we can do now.'

'And if I was wrong?' Will asked.

'Then we play it as a false alarm, go back to the drawing board, and try to work out what to do next. But if you're confident about everything you've seen, it's not worth taking the chance.'

'Yes, I'm confident. This is happening here and now.'

'Alright. We're down to an hour and one minute,' Woods said. 'Which gives us fifty-one minutes to find it before we set off the alarm and start clearing people out. Let's go.'

TWENTY-THREE

While the others began searching the outer perimeter, Will remained inside. He wanted to check every single storage room in the hospital. He tried to move as quickly as he could, without raising the suspicions of any of the staff. After he searched the sixth room on the ground floor, he checked his watch. Forty-one minutes to 9 a.m., thirty-one minutes until Ravi would have to begin the emergency evacuation.

Will knew time was against him, and the search was feeling fruitless. He entered an elevator to go up to the third floor. During the ride up, he climbed onto the hand railing and peered through the maintenance hatch at the top of the lift. Aside from seeing lots of thick cables, and learning how fast the elevator actually moved, he found nothing. When he got off on the third floor, he remembered the episode of ear ringing he'd experienced near the dumpster by the loading dock, and how it'd been much more severe than what he'd heard in the supply cupboard.

Immediately, Will abandoned his plans to search the third-floor storage rooms. He jabbed the down button at least twenty times, until the elevator returned. Back on the ground floor, he hurried through the hospital and out into the loading dock, which was usually quiet before 9 a.m. As he ran down a concrete ramp, he saw the large metal dumpster was no longer in its usual place. Because of its smell, it always remained outside the dock area. Now, however, it was pushed right up against the wall that backed onto the hospital itself. It also normally remained open, so rubbish could be easily tossed inside, but the lid was closed.

Slowing, he crept past the incinerator room, pushing some sealed barrels of medical waste aside. He peered around the loading dock, but couldn't see or hear anyone. Fitting his hands under the dumpster's lid, he tried to lift it, struggling against its weight. The bin was half-filled by bags of rubbish and bits of scrap wood and metal. He used some extra upper body effort and opened it a little further.

Four large metal pipes were secured to the underside of the lid. They were exactly as he'd seen them in his vision yesterday, but instead of being several centimetres long, they were almost half a metre. Each had a digital display strapped to its centre. The timers were counting down, and had just passed 29:00.

Will's entire body trembled. He didn't know what to do with the lid – what if a sudden movement set them off? His eyes watered, and he tried to remain as still as he could, but his arms were shaking with the weight of the lid. Carefully, he lowered it back to its original position. He took a deep breath and checked his phone. It was exactly twenty-eight minutes to 9 a.m.

Taking a few slow steps away from the dumpster, Will called Woods.

'Hey, where are you?' she asked.

'I found them. Four of them, in the dumpster out the—'

Will was grabbed from behind and forced into a powerful chokehold. The arm holding his neck was thick and muscular. He couldn't fight against it. He'd already been panicking while on the call with Woods, so there was very little air left in his lungs. His head went light, and his body went limp, releasing the phone. As it fell, he was thrown face-first into the hard ground. His forehead smashed into the concrete, and he felt the weight of someone on top of him. He tried to inhale, but the pressure on his back was too great. His lungs weren't able to expand. Just when he thought he'd lose consciousness, his arms were pulled back, his wrists bound together with cable ties.

The weight lifted off him. He took a deep breath. His older injuries ached, and his head was bleeding, but he could turn it to the side. His phone was on the ground, still connected to the call with Woods.

'Will? Will, what's going on? Are you there?'

A large black boot slammed down on the phone, crushing it to pieces.

'Get up,' a rough voice demanded.

Will was still trying to catch his breath. He couldn't move. Two hands fisted in his grey hospital shirt, and in less than a second, he was standing with his back to his attacker.

'Who are you?'

'I work here in maintenance,' he said unsteadily. His head throbbed and blood was running into his eyes.

The man said nothing. He pushed Will toward the incinerator room, still clutching the back of his shirt. Will stumbled through the large double doors. His attacker threw him down. With his hands still bound, he wasn't able to break his fall, and landed straight on his right shoulder.

Two powerful hands reached under his armpits and sat him upright. For the first time, Will got a proper look at who he was dealing with. The man wore a tight black t-shirt, his arms rippling with thick, old muscle. His buzz cut showed what was once jet-black hair, now speckled with grey, matching the colour of the stubble on his square chin.

'Who were you talking to on the phone?' he asked, without emotion.

Will didn't respond. The man slapped him hard. The sound of the palm colliding with his cheek rang in his ears and stung his face.

'When I ask a question, you answer!'

'I was just calling my colleague at the hospital,' Will said, in a broken, quiet voice. 'I told you, I work here.'

'You saw what's in the dumpster?' He leaned down and stared directly into Will's eyes.

'Yes,' Will replied nervously. The man, however, seemed content with his answer, and gave a small nod before standing upright.

'I'll be back. If you scream or yell out, I'll put a bullet in your head.'

The man turned and strode out of the incinerator room. Just before he left, Will saw a black handgun tucked down his jeans, sitting in the small of his back.

Will lowered his head. Blood dripped from his forehead to the ground. He had no idea how he was going to get out of this, and no idea how the bombs could be stopped. Every minute was critical, but he wasn't going anywhere.

The man returned to the room with a grin on his face.

'Good. Looks like you didn't touch anything. We don't want them going off too early, now do we?'

As he sauntered back toward Will, footsteps echoed nearby.

'Will, where are you?' Woods called in a whisper.

'Aubrey, get away now!' he shouted. The man struck him in the face again and he slammed back to the ground.

Yanking the handgun from the back of his pants, the man ran out of the incinerator room.

***

The man took Woods by surprise. Before she'd realised what was happening, he had a gun levelled at her chest. She brushed her jacket back, exposing her own.

'Don't even think about it,' he said. 'Hands above your head, now!'

Woods froze, but quickly snapped out of it and obeyed the direction.

'Who are you?' she asked.

'You're not in a position to be asking questions,' he said. 'You're obviously a cop. Walk toward me and take off your jacket. Slowly, got it?'

Woods nodded and removed her blazer, leaving it on the ground as she approached him.

'Got a radio?'

'Yes.'

'Where?'

'It's clipped to the side of my belt.'

'Take it off and drop it. Who else knows you're here?'

'Just Will. Is he okay?'

'He'll live. For now.'

Woods unclipped her radio and placed it on the ground.

'Handcuffs?'

She reached into the pouch on the back of her belt.

'Uh-uh, I'll do that. Turn around and walk back toward me.'

Woods took slow, careful steps backward until the man's hand touched her shoulder, the tip of his gun pressing into her back. She shuddered.

'Stay still,' he said, as he reached into the pouch and removed the set of steel cuffs. He snapped them tightly onto her wrists, before removing her gun from its holster and throwing it to the ground.

'Walk toward the room straight ahead. The gun will stay pushed into your back, so don't do anything stupid.'

The moment Woods entered the room, she saw Will, on the ground with his face dripping blood.

'I'm so sorry,' he said, tears filling his eyes.

'Be quiet,' the man said. He kicked Woods in the back of her knees, and she buckled. With lightning speed, the man lifted Will off the ground one-handed, sitting the two back-to-back. He pulled another set of cable ties out of his pocket, then threaded them through Woods's handcuffs and Will's existing cable ties.

'Always be over-prepared,' he muttered.

Nineteen minutes to detonation.

TWENTY-FOUR

The man paced around the incinerator room, studying his captives.

'So, here we are. A hospital maintenance worker and a cop, snooping around the loading dock. Who wants to explain all this, huh?'

Woods tapped Will on the wrist, indicating she would take the lead.

'Yes, I'm a cop,' she said. 'I'm picking up some medical records for a case I'm working on. Will's my boyfriend, and he works here.'

'Meeting up in the loading dock? That's a little sneaky of you both.'

'I guess.' She shrugged, trying to downplay the perilous situation they were in.

The man reached down and felt Woods's trouser pocket. He pulled out her police ID.

'Aubrey Woods, detective. Well, you two are going to stay right here, and after a few last-minute touches, I'll be gone.'

'What are you going to do?' Woods asked.

'Ask your boyfriend – he knows all about it,' the man said, and chuckled to himself. 'Go on, tell her what's under the dumpster lid. It won't make a difference now.'

'Bombs, I assume,' Will muttered.

'Correct. Well, a galvanised steel pipe explosive, to be specific, filled with enough gunpowder and chlorate to do some nasty damage to this place. Quite easy to make if you know what you're doing.'

'Why not just shoot us?' Woods asked.

'Please, I was never going to shoot you. Why would I risk the sound of a gunshot? It's for emergencies only, and you'll be finished soon, anyway.'

The man strode over to Will and grabbed him by the front of his blood-soaked shirt.

'What I don't appreciate is being bothered by someone snooping around. I might not shoot you, but I'll do what it takes to keep you quiet.'

Laughing, the man brushed the barrel of his gun over Will's face. It was cold, and he winced as it dragged over his cut forehead.

'You know, you can kill a man easily with just the tip of a gun. It's nice and quiet, too.'

'Leave him alone!' Woods yelled.

The man snorted. 'No, you'll both stay here,' he said. 'I might even set up another timer for you, so you can watch the display and count how long you have left.'

The man checked his heavy-duty watch and grinned. 'Oh, fifteen minutes to go! It's nearly time.'

Will drew in a deep breath, searching for some courage.

'So, you're going to kill all those innocent people,' he said.

'Innocent people!' the man said. As he leaned down in front of Will, his joyful demeanour disappeared. 'There's nothing innocent about anyone in there.'

'Of course there is!' Will said, feeling he no longer had anything left to lose. 'There's children, and—'

The man struck Will again, cutting his lip open. Tears filled the man's eyes.

'Don't you dare start,' he said. 'Everyone in this building is going to die. Consider yourselves lucky – you're in close range, you won't even feel a thing. The people on the upper floors might not be so fortunate. Some will fall, some will be crushed under the debris, but they all deserve it.'

'How could anyone possibly deserve that?' Will asked.

'Neither of you know what I've gone through. How could you? You haven't seen what I've seen, been betrayed by your own government, let down by the healthcare system.' Tears trickled down his cheek, but he slapped himself in the face and grabbed Will by the throat, bringing him inches from his snarl.

'You have no idea what I've gone through!' he bellowed, his hot breath spraying Will's face.

'Tell us, then,' Woods said. 'Help us understand – we want to understand. At least tell us your name.'

She sounded far more confident than Will would've expected, given the situation, and he immediately caught on to her goal. In less than five minutes, Ravi would pull the fire alarm. He didn't know how the man would react to an evacuation, but unless something happened, they would all be killed regardless.

'Just talk to us. You have nothing to lose now, do you?' Will asked, trying to hide his hatred.

The man gritted his teeth and spat at Will.

'My name doesn't matter,' he said. 'My son is dead. He was murdered here, by this very hospital. Do you know what that feels like?'

'No, I don't,' Will said.

'What happened?' Woods asked, doing an excellent job of faking sympathy.

'My ten-year-old boy had cancer. Now he's dead, and I'm doing what's right by him. It's as simple as that.'

'I don't understand,' she said. Will could see her trying to calculate how much longer they had until Ravi started the evacuation.

'It was just me and him. He was sick, really sick, for days and days. I brought him here to work out what was wrong, but the doctors sent us home. Told me they found nothing. But I know what really happened – they took one look at us and decided we weren't worth it.'

The man paused, visibly struggling to control himself.

'Yesterday, I spoke to someone here. The administration manager. She told me the hospital wasn't responsible, that the doctors did everything correctly, that they did the best they could. She lied right to my face!'

His control slipped.

'I'm a war veteran!' he roared. 'How could they treat us like that?'

'I'm really sorry that happened,' Woods said. 'But you—'

'He got even worse,' the man interrupted. 'He was so frail. When I brought him back, they told me it was too late. The cancer had spread through his whole body.' He lowered his head and wept. 'A week later, he died.'

'What was his name?' Wood asked.

'You don't need to know!' he barked, wiping his tears away, as his aggressive demeanour quickly returned.

'How could you kill all these people who've done nothing to you?' Will said, trying to match the man's intensity.

'Done nothing? Haven't you been listening? They killed my son.'

'What about everyone they save? I see all the good done here. Your son wouldn't want you to do this.'

The man rushed over and punched Will in the face.

'Don't you ever talk about my son!' he screamed, and turned on Woods. 'And the same goes for you.' He grabbed her hair and yanked her head backwards, smashing it into Will's, then strode out of the room, mumbling to himself.

'Will, you okay?' she whispered.

'Yeah,' he replied. 'Sorry I got him worked up. I didn't mean to.'

'I know. I don't think you'll be able to reason with him, but it was worth a try. Just hang in there, alright? It's going to be okay.'

Before Will could ask what she meant, the man returned, carrying a duffle bag.

'Everything's in place and looking good,' he said, with a sly grin. 'I'm off. Best of luck.'

As he backed toward the door, a shrill ringing screeched through the loading dock. Ravi had triggered the fire alarm, exactly as planned.

Ten minutes until detonation.

TWENTY-FIVE

Will lifted his aching head, a smile sweeping over his face. The fire alarm was blaring throughout the entire hospital. People would already be filing out. As the ringing continued, he heard a voice over the loudspeaker.

'This is not a drill. There is a fire in the hospital. Please evacuate in an orderly fashion, in accordance with the instructions of the staff. Nursing unit managers, follow regular evacuation protocols. This is not a drill.'

It was Ravi. He must've gained access to the PA system to hurry people out. However, Will's relief was restrained, as he knew they only had ten minutes before the pipe bombs would detonate, and he was still helplessly tied to Woods. Nobody knew where they were, and he couldn't see a way out for either of them – or the hundreds of people who'd take longer than ten minutes to evacuate.

For the first time, Will could detect panic in the man's eyes. Will knew this made him incredibly dangerous, and hoped he didn't have another plan up his sleeve.

'What is this?' he muttered, as though talking to himself, before directing his next question to Will. 'What is this?'

'It's the fire alarm,' Will replied.

'How do I turn it off?'

'You can't. There's no override, it's a safety mechanism. Only the fire brigade can stop it.'

'It isn't too late to give up on all this,' Woods said. 'Deactivate the bombs and just walk away.'

'Shut up!' The man crouched and started smacking the side of his head, mumbling to himself. 'No, no, no, no, no.'

Pulling his gun out again, he stood up, pacing around the incinerator, as if he'd forgotten his two hostages. He was looking more dangerous by the moment. Will wondered if pulling the fire alarm had been a big mistake.

The man slowed. He took a couple of deep breaths and raised the handgun to his eye level. Removing the magazine, he examined it, before checking the chamber. Once he was satisfied, he strode out of the incinerator room and turned left, out of sight. Will knew the layout of the building well enough to realise he was heading to the hospital's rear entrance.

Will flinched at the sound of an echoed bang. Woods shuddered, and they both wrestled with their restraints. The ties only pulled tighter, digging into Will's wrists.

'Will, he's going to go on a rampage in there! And the bombs are still due to go off.'

Will stopped struggling and tried to catch his breath. His wrists were cut, and his head was spinning.

'There must be, what, eight minutes to go?' she said.

'Aubrey, what have we done? We've completely set him off,' Will said, his voice faltering as more blood leaked from his forehead.

'Stop it,' she replied, without hesitation. 'The plan was in place for a reason. If we'd done nothing, the bombs would've gone off anyway. We still have time.'

Suddenly, something occurred to Will. The bomber and the hospital. It was so familiar, as if he'd seen it happen before.

'Come on, let's try to stand up,' Woods said. 'We can't just sit here.'

Will didn't reply.

'Will?' Woods asked, leaning back into him. 'What's wrong?'

Will's head dropped, blood still dripping down his cheeks, as he fell unconscious.

***

When the man stepped through the back entrance of the hospital, he saw nothing but an empty corridor. He raised his gun and let off a round into the ceiling. As dust rained down, he heard screams somewhere nearby, and stalked down the corridor in search of them.

The fire alarm had only been activated moments ago. There would still be plenty of people left for him.

Although he'd only been there a few times, his military training had been so deeply ingrained that he still subconsciously examined every new space he entered. He knew the entry points, the lengths of the corridors, and how they all networked together to form the completed hospital.

Today, he had a personal mission on his mind. Revenge. All he was interested in was taking out as many people as he could. With limited ammunition, he'd target the medical staff, who had failed his son.

He cursed himself for throwing the cop's gun away. There was no point going back for it, though. He'd make do with the pistol in his hand – take out a few of the bastards, and let the bombs eliminate the rest.

He had seventeen bullets. He'd kill them, one by one, until he'd spent all his rounds.

Gun hanging by his side, he crept through a ward, pulling curtains back in search of his first target. Although the fire alarm was still blaring, the ward seemed quiet. The beds were empty, and there were no doctors or nurses in sight. He forced himself to remain patient.

On his way toward the front of the hospital, he approached a long corridor lined with closed doors. All his training told him that it was a hazard – a fatal funnel – with no cover, and no room for error. In a military situation, he would've avoided it, but the security guards employed by the hospital were unarmed and no match for him.

At the end of the corridor, a shadow appeared. He expected a body to follow soon after. The long-distance shot would be difficult with a handgun, but he raised it, took a deep breath, and waited.

A fraction of a second later, a female doctor stepped across the hallway. Doctor Michelle Stone. In the panic of the evacuation, she hadn't noticed the gun directed at her.

The man pressed the trigger. His bullet struck Doctor Stone's arm as several screams sounded nearby. Gripping her wounded arm, she dropped to the floor, blood staining her crisp white coat. The man fired again, this time missing.

Doctor Stone's head snapped up. A look of terrified surprise and pain poured over her face. She crawled back the way she came, dragging herself out of sight.

The man sprinted down the corridor, lost in a blind rage. The only thought in his mind was of finding the doctor and ending the job. He skidded around the corner, gun raised, promising himself he wouldn't miss again. The floor was lined with droplets of blood.

Too easy, he thought. Follow the trail and finish her.

Over the ringing of the fire alarm, he called out to the hiding doctor, taunting her as he stalked down the hall.

'Come out, come out! There's no point in hiding now.'

The trail of blood stopped outside a closed door at the end of the corridor. The man tried the handle, but it was locked. He raised his boot and kicked, just once. The door flew open.

His target sat on an examination bed, petrified. He raised his pistol, ready to take the killing shot.

From the corner of his eye, he saw several dark figures approaching. He spun to the left. A team of six tactical police officers clattered down the hall, heavy-duty automatic rifles pointed dead on the centre mass of his body. They wore full black overalls, face coverings, and helmets. He backed away from the door.

'Don't move!' one officer yelled.

The man ran back down the empty corridor. Even with the fire alarm blaring in his ear, he could hear the team chasing after him. He sprinted as hard as he could, back to the loading dock, where the bombs were still awaiting detonation.

The man burst through the door and raced toward the dumpster. He flipped the lid open, exposing the explosives.

***

Woods heard the commotion of the man panting and swearing to himself, but she was still bound on the floor, with Will unconscious behind her.

'Will, come on! Please wake up!' She rocked back and forth, trying to bring him back to consciousness.

Through the open door, she saw the group of tactical police storm into the loading dock, and challenge the man standing by the dumpster.

'Drop the gun and get on the ground, now!'

The man laughed.

'On the ground!' one officer repeated. 'I'm warning you – we'll shoot.'

'Well, that won't do you any good,' the man replied, smirking.

'I won't tell you again!'

'You have more problems than just me. Go ahead and take a look.'

He pointed toward the dumpster, where the four pipe bombs were on display.

'You see that?' he asked. 'Timers. I've brought them forward, so now you have… let's see' —he glanced over to the displays— 'sixty-five seconds before they take out most of the hospital.'

The tactical supervisor swallowed. 'You'll blow yourself up too.'

Another officer cried out, 'Turn them off! There's no way out for you.'

'Oh, I don't care about that anymore,' the man said, and raised his handgun.

All six officers opened fire. The man fell to the ground in a hail of bullets, blood pooling around him.

'Help!' Woods called. 'In here!'

Two of the tactical officers ran toward the dumpster, while the other four sprinted into the incinerator room. Once they saw Woods, they lowered their guns, and hurried to remove the handcuffs and untie her and the still-unconscious Will.

'Is he okay?' one asked Woods.

'He's been knocked out, and he's lost a bit of blood.'

The tactical supervisor nodded. 'I'll carry him. We have to get out of here. We only have about thirty seconds left, and the bombs can't be deactivated that quickly.'

'There are still people inside!' another officer called.

'There's no time – we need to go.'

As the officers finished removing the cable ties, Will slowly came back into consciousness.

'Will!' Woods gasped. 'Quick, stand up. We have to leave!'

'Wait,' he said, groggily.

'We have less than thirty seconds until those bombs go off! Just run, now!'

'No, I can disarm them.'

With that, Will wrestled out of the light grip of the officer who'd helped him stand, and ran toward the open dumpster, jumping over the man's body.

'Will, stop!' Woods yelled. 'Don't touch them!'

The officers ran after Will, but it was too late. By the time they caught up with him, he was at the dumpster, and the timers were showing fourteen seconds to detonation.

'Just go! Get as far away as you can,' said the supervisor, grabbing Woods by the arm and pulling her back.

'Will! What are you doing?'

Without hesitation, Will moved the blue and red wires aside, and yanked the yellow wires out of the bombs.

The displays on all four timers ticked down to zero.

TWENTY-SIX

Will took a deep breath. Slowly, he removed the heavy caps from each of the four pipes, placing them on the ground beside the dumpster. When he was satisfied the bombs were disarmed, he shouted back to Woods and the tactical team, who were about a hundred metres away.

'It's okay. It's safe!'

They stared back at Will. Almost thirty seconds had passed since the explosives were due to detonate.

Woods moved first, running back toward Will.

'You're insane!' she yelled. You know that, don't you?'

Will just shrugged.

'Are you sure it's safe?' she asked.

'They won't explode, but I'd imagine it's still best to section off the area until they've been properly disposed of.'

The tactical team caught up with Woods, pulling off their helmets and face coverings.

'You crazy bastard,' one said, shaking his head.

'How'd you know what you were doing?' another asked.

'I just did,' Will replied.

As the supervisor began issuing directions to his team, Woods took Will by the arm.

'Come on, let's go find Ravi. We should get you checked out, too – that cut on your forehead's looking pretty bad.'

She led him around the hospital, toward the front, where a mass of people were waiting for the alarm to stop, completely unaware of what had just transpired.

As they made their way through the crowd, Ravi spotted them and waved. Seeing Will's head, he pulled a first aid kit from the back of an ambulance and brought it over with him.

'Geez, what happened to you?' he said, helping Will sit on the edge of a garden bed.

'It's all over, Ravi,' Will said. 'Tell someone to turn that alarm off, it's giving me a headache.'

A few people stared at the large gash on Will's forehead. Ravi began cleaning and dressing the wound, as Woods took a seat next to him.

'What the hell happened in there?' Ravi asked. 'I saw the police charge in, but I had no idea what was going on.'

'Well, you pulled the alarm at just the right time,' Will said, wincing as Ravi applied pressure to his head.

'You found a bomb, then?'

'We found it, alright. Four of them.'

'We ran into the perp too,' Woods said. 'He tied us up and knocked us around. For a moment there, I didn't think we'd make it, but it's over now. The perp's dead, and somehow, Will deactivated the bombs before they went off.'

'You what?' Ravi asked.

'Yeah. I knew what I was doing.'

'How could you have possibly known how to disarm a bomb?' Woods asked. 'You scared the hell out of me. One minute you're unconscious, the next you're ripping wires out of live explosives. What was that all about?'

Will nodded. He knew he had some explaining to do. 'Just before I passed out, something clicked. I remembered the dreams

I'd had, back when I was recovering here in the hospital. I realised they weren't just ordinary dreams; they were my first visions. I saw the explosions, and the carnage they'd left. Once, I was assembling the bombs myself – arming and disarming them. Thinking about it, I realised it couldn't just be a coincidence. I knew I could deactivate the bombs, because I'd seen them before.'

'Well, it was insane,' Woods said, 'but you saved my life, along with hundreds of people in that hospital.'

'That's pretty incredible,' Ravi said, as he rummaged through the first aid kit. 'Although we're still no closer to making sense of how you can see what you do.'

'Honestly, I'm not sure we ever will,' he replied. 'But that's okay. After everything that's happened, maybe I don't I need to know why.'

Ravi poured saline over Will's head, and the stinging sensation made him flinch.

'So, the bomber,' Ravi said. 'What was his story?'

'He was just a very sick and very disgruntled person,' he said, clenching his teeth.

Woods rose to her feet. 'Yeah, and I'm going to find out more about him if I can.' Turning, she disappeared into the crowd.

When he'd finished bandaging Will's head, Ravi packed up the kit.

'You'll need stitches for that. We'll get it sorted once the hospital reopens.'

'Sure,' Will said. 'Also, after the fire alarm went off, the man ran out with a gun. I don't know if he hurt anyone.'

'Oh, no,' Ravi groaned. 'See, that's why I was worried about pulling the alarm!'

'Hey, it was a risk, and we knew that, but it might've saved the whole hospital. Without it, I probably wouldn't have had the chance to disarm the bombs. Luckily, the police ended up untying us just in time. Actually – why were they even there?'

Ravi shrugged. 'No idea. I really hope no one's hurt. I think we cleared most people from the ground floor, but I'm going to go back and look around.'

Standing, he made his way to the entrance of the hospital.

'It's definitely safe to go in?' he called back.

'Definitely.'

***

A few minutes later, Woods rejoined Will, taking in the warm sun while they watched a convoy of police run crime scene tape around the perimeter of the hospital. Judging by the mutters from the gathered onlookers, it irritated many of them, until a large truck arrived on the scene, followed by two fire engines. Then, the crowd's mood shifted to a nosy interest. The fire brigade, along with the team from the Rescue and Bomb Disposal Unit, began putting on protective clothing. This piqued the curiosity of the crowd even further.

A middle-aged, stern-looking police officer, who appeared to have taken charge of the scene, stood up in front of the onlookers with a megaphone in hand.

'Ladies and gentlemen, there has been an incident at the hospital,' he said. 'Although the situation is fully under control, we need you all to stay out here. If you have loved ones still inside, I can assure you they're safe – we just can't have anyone else inside for now. Thank you for your patience.'

Loud chatter filled the crowd as he switched off his megaphone. A few other uniformed police officers spotted Woods, and ran over to check up on her.

'I'm fine, don't worry,' she said, brushing them off. 'You must have plenty of work to do.'

'Okay. We'll talk later in the debrief, when this is all cleared up,' one said, before they all hurried off to help manage the onlookers.

'How am I going to get out of this one?' Will asked. 'I assume they're going to ask me how I did it.'

'Tell them whatever you'd like. Make something up. We both know what happened, and you saved a lot of lives today.'

Will nodded. 'Why were the tactical police there? I mean, how did they know?'

'I called them in,' she said. 'As soon as you mentioned "four of them" in a dumpster, I knew what you meant.'

'I could've been wrong.'

'You weren't. Besides, after everything that's happened, I promised myself I wouldn't ignore you again.'

'Thanks, Aubrey.'

'No, thank you. Now rest up – I'm going to go check back in on the situation.'

Woods left again, while Will stayed on the edge of the garden bed, thinking about how lucky he and everyone else had just gotten. He couldn't help feeling a little sorry for the bomber. The man had clearly been sick. His military service had probably left him with PTSD, and that, coupled with the recent loss of his son, must've tipped him over the edge. It was no excuse for what he'd intended to do, but part of Will wished he could've received help a long time ago.

After about ten minutes, Woods returned and sat back down next to Will.

'Things are going well back there,' she said. 'I just went and spoke with the disposal team, and you did properly deactivate the bombs. They're just packing up what's left.'

'And the man?'

'He was wearing his old army tags under his shirt. Francis

Agar, ex-Special Forces Sergeant. We just received some intel from the Army, which said he spent a few years working in a bomb disposal unit in Iraq. While he was on tour, his wife died in a car accident, so he was discharged to look after his son. And, well... everything he said about his son was true.'

'That's really sad.'

'It is. By all accounts, he was an experienced, professional, and dedicated soldier. But I guess everyone has their breaking point.'

Neither spoke for a minute, as Will reflected on everything that'd happened.

'So, what now?' he asked, finally breaking the silence.

'Well, the Rescue and Bomb Disposal Unit will stay here, along with the local uniformed police, to make sure the hospital can go back to normal as soon as possible. Francis Agar's body will be taken to the morgue. Most people will never know what happened today, or just how many lives could've been lost. They'll keep the whole thing quiet. There's no need to create unnecessary fear – he was a lone attacker, and not part of a terrorist organisation.'

'Sounds like it's all under control, then.'

'Yeah,' Woods said. 'You know, I think you should give the victim group another chance. With everything that's happened, you have a lot to talk about. What do you say?'

'I think I'd like that. I just hope I don't give them all another scare,' Will said. He and Woods shared a small, short-lived laugh, before he went quiet, cut off by the wave of emotions still crashing over him.

'I guess it's back to work for both of us,' he said.

'Yeah, until the next disaster. I'm sure you'll see something new before long.'

'Stay by your phone,' Will said, as he stood from the edge of the garden bed and looked back at Woods. 'I just might be in touch.'

The End.

Shawline Publishing Group Pty Ltd
www.shawlinepublishing.com.au

More great Shawline titles can be found here:

New titles also available through Books@Home Pty Ltd.
Subscribe today - www.booksathome.com.au